..."But we don't want to invite trouble by interacting with people," Lang emphasized, looking Natasha in the eyes. "What if they know that the Russians are the ones that attacked? What if one of us slips up and speaks Russian?" He paused and let the questions answer themselves. "No. Peter is right. Let's just avoid people and look for a route that avoids contact as much as possible."

"But we're Americans," Natasha whimpered.

"No, we're not, Natasha. At least not to these people. We have no country," Lang replied...

# WICK 3:
# Exodus

By
# Michael Bunker
With
Chris Awalt

Wick 3: Exodus

© Copyright 2013 by Michael Bunker and Chris Awalt

ISBN: 9781482797763

FIRST PRINTING

*All rights reserved. No portion of this book may be reproduced in any form, except for brief quotations in reviews, without the written permission of the author.*

**Cover Design:**
Jason Gurley
http://www.jasongurley.com

**Formatting:**
Stewart Stonger
http://design.nourishingdays.com/

For information on Michael Bunker, or to read his blog:
**http://www.michaelbunker.com**

To contact Michael Bunker, please write to:

M. Bunker
1251 CR 132
Santa Anna, Texas 76878

# WICK 3:
## Exodus

By
# Michael Bunker
With
## Chris Awalt

**Fiction Disclaimer:**
This book is a work of fiction. Names, characters, places, and events either are the products of the author's imagination, or are used fictitiously. Any resemblance to actual events, locales, or persons, living or dead, is entirely coincidental.

# Acknowledgements

*This one is for all you awesome WICK fans out there who have given us such a fun ride. We're happy to give you the next "knot" in the story. Without all the fantastic support, there is no way the series would have had such great success. Thank you all. As always, thank you to our family and friends. Thank you again to all of our beta readers and the other editors as well.*

# Chapter 1
# Exodus

At the bottom of the hill they turned west for a moment and then followed along the banks of a stream until they found a fallen tree that formed a natural bridge—large and solid enough to carry their weight as they traversed the stream's width. With Peter in the lead, they hiked through the Forest Preserve, heading generally in a southwesterly direction, making their way by the angle of the sun in the fall sky. The walking was rough because the snow was high, but they settled into a rhythm that kept them pushing forward with firm conviction.

They did their best to stay cloaked under a cover of trees because they had no way of knowing whether they might be spotted by the swarm of drones that had, just hours before, swept in and laid waste to the town behind them. They were survivors and, from the stain left on the earth back in their village, it was clear to them that whoever had ordered the drone strike did not intend for there to be *any* survivors. Although manageable, the cold was persistent with its stinging rebuke, and it forced them to keep moving to stay warm.

They walked, occupying themselves with thoughts of how their lives had come to this, and what might lie before them. Everything was going to change now. These three were free human beings, perhaps for the first time in their lives, but that very thought carried a terror all its own. History is replete with examples of brave men and women who found peace in the depths of a prison. One need only utter the names of John Bunyan, Mandela, Ghandi, Bobby Sands, or Vaclav Havel to understand this. However, there was also the story of the Israelites following Moses out of Egypt only to turn to newer and more willful forms of enslavement to suggest that, once the bonds of the physical have been lifted, the spirit and the mind still remain to be tamed.

Unfettered now from entangling alliances, oaths, and contracts signed by strangers on their behalf before they were even born, the three traveled toward the unknown, not knowing yet how they would respond to trials they would meet along their way. Emerson wrote that, when you travel, your giant travels with you. Now Peter, Lang, and Natasha quietly pondered whether they were prepared, whether they would survive, whether they were up to the task of carrying the giants resting on their shoulders as they trudged through the snow towards...

*What?*

There was no answer to that question. At least for now.

Peter's plan had been roughly sketched long ago through talks with Lev Volkhov, the wise old leader who had foreseen the trouble they now faced. They would head towards Amish country in Pennsylvania. The reasons for this had not been entirely clear to the younger Lang and Natasha, but those reasons were actually quite simple in their conceptualization. The plans were founded on a belief that the three would fare better in Amish country than anywhere else. It was that simple.

Their small town and provincial ways, as well as their ignorance of the means and patterns of modern life among the "English" (which is the term used by the Amish for all outsiders—since we are speaking of them) would serve as a two-edged sword in this journey. First, they would make Peter, Lang, and Natasha more vulnerable to the conditions in the wider American landscape. Second, they would explain away any idiosyncrasies of behavior once they became enmeshed among another group that had been born and raised in an insular society. Both considerations argued for their plan. No matter which way the sword cut, it suggested they should go to Amish country. If they could get to the Amish they would have a better chance to survive. Or at least that was the hope, Peter thought, as he looked up and along the ridgeline of a mountain in the distance and set his chin against the cold of the coming climb.

Had the three travelers been born In Los Angeles or Des Moines, or almost anywhere else in America other than their insulated hamlet, they might have wondered about the logic of the plan. Why go to the Amish during a time of war? Aren't they pacifists? Won't they be the first to meet their end? This seems like a reasonable objection. However, there is a supposition behind that thought that had to be addressed. History tells a story of the pacifist Amish that contradicts the implications of the argument. The bare essential of that history is that, pacifist or not, the Amish have been around for more than five-hundred years. Most of those years have been lived out in the most violent places and times in the history of civilization. Napoleon and his armies had come and gone... as had the Russian Empire, the Japanese Empire, and most of the British Empire... but the Amish still abide. Whether one attributed this fact to the protections offered by their religious faith, or the fact that, as a community, they took care of their own, or to a latent human conscience that respected their passivity and way of life, the fact remains that they were survivors. Their pacifism and faith protected them like the Alps protected Swiss neutrality. Being a student of history Volkhov understood this

The old sage had not known how the war would unfold, but he did know that it would be brutal and ugly for the physically-pampered and mentally-weak Americans, who were notoriously unprepared for what war could be like if it occurred on their own soil. Volkhov would often point out that the total number of American deaths by war during the American Civil War was 150% of those experienced during World War II, this despite the fact that the total deaths by combat in that earlier war were only 75% of those in the latter. The same relationship was evident in a comparison of, say, the American Revolutionary War and the Korean War, with the corresponding numbers being 70% and 24%. This is not even to mention how untrained and ill-educated Americans are when it comes to the things needed for survival and for facing hardship during such a conflict breaking out in the homeland.

The point in war, Volkhov was fond of saying, is to stay alive, and too many Americans miss that point when war occurs in the streets of their own towns. As he climbed, Peter looked over his shoulder at his younger colleagues, who were at that moment lost in deep thoughts of their own but struggling gamely onward through the snow, and he decided that, if he had anything to do with it, they would not be subject to such a failure.

Peter had noted when he'd been packing their go-bags for the exodus that, while their provisions were in good condition, he couldn't say the same for himself. He'd leaned down a little too quickly to lift up a box and stood a little too awkwardly to set the box on the table and felt a sharp pain in his back, the signs of aging that had plagued him more and more over the last several years. He had, throughout his life, participated in extensive training, and he'd even been an instructor in the charm school's *SERE* course for two years, but that was when he'd been quite a bit younger and in a lot better shape. Search, Evasion, Resistance, and Escape training and experience would help, he thought, but he was out of practice and (if truth be told) out of shape. Like many people his age, he had become soft and addicted to his creature comforts. For his younger colleagues, they had youth, but that youth was laced with inexperience. *If age but could, if youth but knew.* He tightened his jaw and thought to himself that they would have to combine their wits and abilities if they were to make it out of this alive.

\* \* \* \*

Peter knew that it was not a great plan. It might not even be a *good* one, but it was all they had. What they knew with certainty is that they could not make it through the winter on their own. If they'd stayed in Warwick, they would be dead already, and if they were caught by either side in the war that seemed to be around and upon them, things would not go well for them. If any of them were tortured or even closely questioned by either side, they would inevitably be found out, and all the protestations in the world wouldn't help. The body of truth lies dead in the ditch in almost any war, a casualty of necessity and fear. Simply by virtue of their being Russian, they would be suspected by anyone who caught them. *What happened next would not be pretty*, Peter thought. *Especially for Natasha.*

It is an interesting irony that in those cultures and times when women have been *less* equal, they have been *more* honored, treasured, and protected from war. *Perhaps I am old-fashioned*, Peter thought, grabbing a limb to steady himself as he stepped over a fallen log, *but I know this to be true.* Despite what many modern folks have come to believe, history reveals that when the artificial veil of civility is rent, and when the ghostly wisps and remnants of chivalry and ancient patriarchy are eradicated altogether and thrown to the ground during times of general upheaval... well, let us just say that throughout antiquity, and in every place and every time, women have fared the worst in times of war. Men are usually granted the dignity of *just* being killed, Peter thought.

He scratched his beard and glanced up into the sun. The more liberated the culture, the more horrible has been the treatment of women during and after the culture crumbles. Well, Natasha would have to be protected and watched over, he thought. *She has no family left... that I know of.* He looked around and watched the young woman walking behind him, and saw the lines of concern etched on her face. He determined that, even if she didn't want it, he would stand in the breach and protect her.

All three of the travelers had some training. All three had gone through mandatory classes on spycraft, weapons, and tactics. But they would learn now that there is a universe of difference between theory and the real world. Peter just hoped that the learning curve would not be too steep, and that the course in harsh reality wouldn't kill them.

The air was crisp and cold and the sky was the bluest of blue— the kind of blue that seems impossible except by contrast. Every now and then a sharp breeze would blow and snow would fall from overhead branches where it would lay trapped by pine needles and oak leaves. The snow, blown from the deposits in the trees, would swirl around them and make them uncomfortable, and, on a few occasions, it would crash down upon them, falling into their collars and sliding down their necks, melting from the heat of their bodies and trickling icy cold sludge down their backs in lacy jags, adding impetus to their chill. The cold on their backs mixing with the cold in their feet sent jolts through their systems to keep them moving ahead.

Coming over a low rise, they saw in the distance a small camp. They were far enough away and downwind so they hunkered down and watched the camp awhile from afar, wondering silently what they should do. The camp seemed to consist of a few families, and they were huddled around a roaring fire, their three large camping tents arranged in a triangle around the fire with the door flaps opening inward, toward the blaze.

Two of the campers, a man and a woman, were arguing loudly, and hints of words and voices tumbled through the icy air toward the hikers. They seemed to be spouses, the man and the woman, but it wasn't entirely clear from the snippets of sound that reached the trio hiding along the ridge what the point of their argument was. Perhaps she was insisting on equality in the camping chores, or maybe he was blaming her for their current horrendous state. Whatever was their contention, it was clear that they blamed each other–as if either could have held back the uncertainty that now approached them. Pulling together in times of utter peril is a sign that the peril is understood and embraced. These people had no idea what they were in for, but they had camping gear and survival food. They thought they had prepared for occasions such as this, but now, as they argued in the cold, they found that they were woefully mistaken.

Peter turned to Natasha and Lang and put his finger to his lips, before whispering to them. "Obviously, these are some people who decided to 'bug out.' That's the term used by *preppers* or survivalists who are of the opinion that they can rush out into the woods when things collapse and they'll be okay. Volkhov purchased dozens of books that spoke of, or even encouraged, this phenomenon. He said that many Americans anticipated a major collapse of their society, but they were deceived in their ideas about how best to deal with it. Millions of people made rudimentary plans to escape the cities and towns, heading into the wilderness, but most of them had little or no training, let alone knowledge of what it would be like to live out here. They did not consider that there were millions of people, just like them, thinking the same thing. This will make things tougher for us."

Peter looked down on the campers and shook his head. "Most of these people are untrained and unpracticed, and their fantasies of wilderness survival will turn to nightmares within days. It will not end well for them. But, some of the people we might run into are militia types and hard-core survivalists. These families here do not look wise or well trained at all. The other kinds—the woodsmen and *real* survivalists... they will have sentries and possibly scouts. We wouldn't have been able to walk up on this ridge like this without alerting them. They will be trained. Some might be benevolent, but others will be anarchists or criminally-minded. Many will be looking for trouble, for a fight. We are better off avoiding all of them."

Natasha chewed on the end of her glove, her eyes searching the scene in front of them. "Maybe they can help us?" she said, her voice betraying hope as well as innocence.

"No Natasha, we mustn't think that way," Lang said, whispering softly, "One mistake and we could be done for. One individual or group that suspects us or is wary of us, or perhaps is just looking to steal and loot their way to survival, and we could all be killed. You heard the radio back at the plant before the EMP. Our world has changed, but *their* world," he indicated with his hand the group in the clearing below and beyond that the wider countryside, "*their* world has changed even more. We have to be smart, like Peter says."

Lang reached over and touched Natasha lightly on her arm, and let his hand rest there a minute until she looked at him with understanding. He sympathized with her fears and even her natural tendency to trust and hope for the best, but that type of naiveté would have to be one of the first casualties of this conflict. "I agree with Peter. We need to avoid people at all costs. I'm already worried because we're walking out in the snow, leaving a trail behind us. There's nothing we can do about that, except try to track close to the trees and rocks. When we can get up on those rocks or exposed land, we do so. We stay midway up the hills and the mountains. Not in the valley, where we can be seen from above, and not on the peaks where we can be seen from below, but halfway up, as much as we are able, all of the time.

"But we don't want to invite trouble by interacting with people," Lang emphasized, looking Natasha in the eyes. "What if they know that the Russians are the ones that attacked? What if one of us slips up and speaks Russian?" He paused and let the questions answer themselves. "No. Peter is right. Let's just avoid people and look for a route that avoids contact as much as possible."

"But we're Americans," Natasha whimpered.

"No, we're not, Natasha. At least not to these people. We have no country," Lang replied.

"Lang's right," Peter said, "we need to go over this rise and stay hidden from them or anyone else like them." He looked into the bright blue sky and judged the time. "We'll keep our eyes open and stop every fifty yards or so to look out and around us. Each of us should be watching and aware of our surroundings all of the time. Listen and look. Remember all of the training we did back in the shed at the water plant. Remember what you learned when you were in school. Keep moving and constantly be aware. We'll stop regularly and check our surroundings so that we don't walk into a trap."

Natasha looked back down over the impromptu camp and she wondered what would happen to these people. Whatever it was, she feared that it would not be good. They seemed to be heedless of any real danger. They acted as if they were just on a camping trip; as if things were going to get better in a few days; as if they could all go home soon. Perhaps if they'd seen their homes, families, and friends wiped off the map by a handful of drones, as these three had, or if they knew that there was no home to go back to, they'd have a little different perspective. As it was, the children ran and sang and shouted and threw snowballs, and the parents just sat looking dead-eyed into the fire... all except, that is, for the one couple that screamed and shouted at one another, each unsatisfied with their situation and blaming the other... each hoping that the other would somehow make it all better.

* * * *

The walk proceeded, and the trio made good time, keeping to their plan. Not too long after they passed the last group of campers, they spied another man walking along the crest of a ridge. He was silhouetted against the sky and was scampering over the rocks heading who knows where. They watched as the man leapt over something in his path and came down on a branch at the top of the ridge that sent a crackling echo down the mountain. He sank down in the snow as the branch gave way beneath his feet.

They stopped, hidden well in the trees, as they watched the man disappear over the ridge. Peter pulled out his map and partially unfolded it across his knee and knelt in the snow. He compared the map to the compass, and he nodded his head in the direction that they should go.

"We need to head towards Carbondale. That ought to let us avoid the worst of the towns and highways, although we'll inevitably have to deal with some of it. On the track we're following, hopefully we'll cross Highway 17 sometime this evening. We need to be across that highway and well clear of it by darkfall. We don't want to stop or camp anywhere near roads or people." Peter traced the intended route with his finger on the map so his two companions could follow.

On their way again, they benefited by not having to cross fence lines or private property. Being in the Forest Preserve had its advantages. As they walked, they noticed in the distance the occasional plume of smoke, heard the random blast of gunfire, but they stayed well clear of any sign of humans, and, in time, they found themselves walking with a single-mindedness that comes from being alone in the wide open spaces.

# Chapter 2
# Mistakes

Mistakes are part of the learning curve, and sometimes they are fatal. Sometimes, for some unknown reason, they could very well have been fatal, but are not. Rounding the corner of a stand of trees almost too thick to walk through, Lang saw him first. Looking up to watch a flock of birds shoot out into the wide blue sky, Lang caught a glimpse of a black coat behind the thick brown branches.

Seated in the trees, with a scoped deer rifle pointed directly at the three refugees from Warwick, a young man sat accompanied by a woman who was huddled next to him in the cold. The two, perilously balanced in the crook of a branch, cowered behind a second limb. Even given his superior position, Lang could see that the man's hands shook as he pointed the gun first at Lang, then at Peter, then back at Lang again. Peter and Natasha did not see the man at first, as they fought through the branches, and Lang had to alert them, tapping Peter on the arm and indicating toward the gunman in the trees.

"Okay, okay, okay..." Lang said loudly, but calmly, bringing his hands up to show that he was unarmed. As he did this, Peter, and then Natasha, looked up and saw the man with the gun, and the woman behind him. Natasha instinctively dropped to the ground as if she were on fire. She brought her hands up as best she could into the air, though her face remained buried in the snow.

The quick motion spooked the gunman, and with a terrified squeal more than a shout he hollered for the trio to "freeze!" which they all did instantly. Natasha steeled her nerves and looked up into the gunman's eyes as Peter raised his hands slowly, and Lang tried to clear his thoughts and take in a fuller picture of what was going on.

*The man is not going to shoot*, Lang thought. *Not unless he is provoked.* The young man with the gun was scared, his hands shook, and the gun shook with them. Lang determined that he wasn't a killer and he wouldn't shoot them on purpose, judging from the look in his eye and the uncertainty with which he held them through the scope. *He might kill one of us on accident, though.*

"Easy there," Lang said, firmly. "Easy with the gun, pal. We're unarmed. Just take your finger off the trigger for a second, and let's talk. We don't want anyone getting hurt because a muscle twitches in all this excitement."

It was not true that they were *completely* unarmed. Peter still had the Ruger 9mm pistol in the pocket of his coat, but the man with the rifle didn't know that.

The man took his finger off the trigger, actually moving his head from behind the scope and looking at the trigger guard to see if his gloved finger was clear. He wasn't planning on shooting anyone... this Lang knew, and the knowledge allowed him to relax his body slightly.

"Easy there, and thank you for not shooting us." Lang didn't move, and made no motion as if he were going to approach. *No need to be foolish*, however certain he was that the man was harmless, at least in his intentions.

Lang concentrated and put on the best New England accent he could muster, though it wasn't great. "Okay, pal. We're just moving through, here. We're just trying to get home, and we're unarmed and we're not going to hurt anybody. We're not even going to approach you. Do you understand me?"

Peter looked at Lang and communicated wordlessly that it would be a simple thing to rush the man, to pull him down from the branch and disarm him, but Lang slowly closed his eyes, silently saying "No." The two men agreed without saying a word.

The gunman nodded, and the woman next to him huddled closer behind him, as if she were a little less sure of the group's lack of harmful intent. "Just keep moving, man!" he shouted. "Don't make me *shoot* anyone!" He tried to make the words sound ominous and threatening, but Lang could hear the desperate uncertainty in his voice.

"We don't want you to shoot anyone either, bro," Lang said, calmly. "We're just going to walk on. You are welcome to come with us, if you want. We're heading towards Pennsylvania."

"Yeah?" the man said, with a voice that suddenly betrayed a hint of a sneer. "Well, you can *have* that!" He looked at them as if they would understand, but they didn't. "I wouldn't go anywhere near the highway if I were you. It's a bloodbath over there." This seemed to be all he was willing to give them as far as explanation, as if his reasons were too painful to discuss. He rattled his gun again. "You guys keep walking or I'll shoot, I swear!" There was a little more certainty this time, seen in the steadying of the gun.

"Okay, man," Lang said, nodding his head as he reached down to help Natasha lift herself out of the snow. He pulled on her with one hand and she was able to rise up. She dusted the snow off her coat and shook her legs as she did. Lang kept his other hand up, and he whispered to Natasha to quit dusting herself and raise her hands. She did so and then the trio backed slowly away. As soon as they were thirty feet or so past the shooter, they began moving faster, and soon they were over the next rise.

"How did you know he was harmless?" Natasha asked, after they had walked for a moment.

"He didn't know what he was doing with that gun. Probably never shot it before. I'm not even sure it was loaded. He just wanted to scare us off. He was scared out of his mind. Probably peed himself."

"I almost did too," Natasha said. "I'm glad he just wanted to frighten us, but I don't understand people. I've never been so afraid in my life... except... maybe when Mikail shot Todd Karagin." Her hands shook as she wiped the melted snow from her face.

"Let's try not to make that mistake again," Peter said, exhaling deeply. He peered ahead into their path with a little more intention.

"You're right, Peter," Lang replied. "But we may not always have warning—and we may not always meet people who don't know which end of the rifle to hold. It'll get tougher when we cross 17 and get into farm country."

"Don't scare me any more than I am already, Lang," Natasha said in protest.

If one listened closely, in that protest could be heard the faintest beginnings of strength.

\* \* \* \*

After several more uneventful hours of walking, Peter called them to a stop with a motion of his hand, and they gathered near a rocky outcropping, and took some time once again to look at the map and compare it with the compass.

"We look to be right in this area," Peter said, circling a section on the map with his finger. "We'll be to Highway 17 in two to three hours if all goes well and the conditions hold up." He turned and looked towards the sun, which was already past its apex, and he held his open hand with the top of his index finger just under the sun facing westward, and then moved his hand downwards four fingers width. He did this several times, then, adding a finger and a half for the hilly terrain, he turned to the others and told them that it seemed to him to be after 1 p.m. "Maybe 1:30," he added.

"Well," Lang said, "I guess we're making good time?"

"Good enough," Peter answered. "When we get near the highway... anywhere within a mile or so, we're going to want to go very slowly and use all of our senses. Like the gunman in the trees said, the highway might be really rough, and we don't want to get caught up in anything."

The three pulled off their packs, and Peter let out a deep sigh when he dropped his to the ground. Of the three, he carried the heaviest load since his pack had the ammo can with the electronic equipment in it. In his mind he lamented his poor physical shape and was kicking himself for not getting more exercise. He felt the cramping in his muscles and reckoned that he would be sore and miserable for the first week of their journey.

They opened the ammo can and pulled out the radio. Peter put in the batteries and tried to tune in anything... anything at all... but all he heard was a vacant and incessant buzzing, the vacuous chorus from all the ambient electricity in the universe.

The three pulled out some of their food, and ate quickly, and Peter ate while standing guard. They all took deep breaths while stomping occasionally to ward off the cold. The three travelers were grateful for the rest, but the cold and the light in the sky gave them reasons to keep moving.

By around 4:30 p.m., they were within a half-mile of the highway and they occasionally heard the random blast or sharp staccato of gunfire. Their current location, because of the thickness of the forest, didn't seem to be a regular path of ingress or egress to the highway, though they had crossed a few places where it had become obvious that masses of people had diverted from the highway as they set off into the forest. Peter told them that he wanted them to stay away from any areas that had become cattle paths for escaping humans.

They moved slower now and with purpose, and, though they were still in the trees, the land was flatter here. There were fewer places for natural cover. They crept along slowly, spread out five to ten yards apart, and each covered and watched a given area. They moved in short hops as they made forward progress slowly.

By 5:30 p.m., they were within fifty yards of the highway and the gunfire had slackened, but only a bit, and now they heard the almost indescribable din of human traffic and misery. The sound was like a wailing that came in around the window on a cold winter's night, a dull cacophony of random shouts and the background sound of feet shuffling and dragging, and the cry of pain and suffering. All-in-all it sounded like one imagines hell to sound, but maybe not down in the very deepest dungeons. Maybe up at the front, near the check-in desk, where they keep things nice for the tourists.

It was entering early evening, and the shadows had grown long, and darkness—not full darkness, but the gloaming—would be upon them soon. They still had not seen any people, but in the distance, over the horizon to the south, they could see smoke rising, and they still heard sporadic gunfire, and they were frightened, though none of them spoke of this fear aloud. Instead, they clenched their jaws and waited for the night.

\* \* \* \*

They approached the highway access road through the trees, and, crawling slowly through the snow, they peered out over the war zone that Highway 17 had become. There were cars on fire, smoke filled the air, and a gauzy fog hung ominously in the ether. Masses of people moved by like soldiers on retreat, solemn in their drudgery. Occasionally, fights broke out in little pockets of disturbance, like dust devils swirling across the desert floor in a sweltering heat.

The trio looked on helplessly as armed gangs opened fire on groups of the marching people. They watched mothers, pulling carts with their children and belongings in them, were pushed to the ground by human animals so that unspeakable acts could be committed. They saw men beaten without provocation or limitation. Gunfire erupted so often, and with such alacrity, that in every way imaginable the three Warwickians could only describe what they were viewing from their vantage point as a massive running gun battle like the kind they had only heard from the safety of their houses when the civil war had broken out in Warwick. Only Natasha had been out in the street during that battle, she swallowed and felt a bitter empathy for the people below.

To the right, northward up the highway but still in their view, a group of men rocked a van loaded with people, and the van eventually overturned, and the men hopped up on it and stomped at the windows until the glass shattered on the occupants inside. They reached their arms into the van and ripped the doors open. They pulled the occupants out, and a few of their victims inside the vehicle escaped and ran up the highway, slipping in the snow, trying to disappear among the crowds. Others, thrown to the ground, lay haplessly while the vandals stomped them and struck them with sticks, rods, or anything else that was at hand. The gang then rifled through the van, stealing whatever they could, before moving on to the next car and repeating the scene.

A high-powered rifle shot rang out from somewhere and one of the gang members fell to the ground, then another shot rang and another thug fell. The crack of the rifles echoed through the clearing like a gong. The surviving gang members took off running northward, leaving their dead comrades behind.

In the distance, there arose a mechanical growl of grinding machinery rolling over the boisterous frenzy, and the three turned their heads to see what could be making such a noise. Eventually they saw it. A line of military vehicles, evidently spared or shielded from the worst of the EMP, crawled clumsily up the highway from the south, and most of the vehicles had guns mounted on the top of them. Soldiers, probably National Guardsmen, perched on top of the vehicles, operating the guns. Quite often though, the gunners disappeared because they ducked down whenever gunfire erupted from some unseen attackers.

The convoy moved slowly but did not stop for anything, and groups of people ran alongside, pawing at the metal of the vehicles. Occasionally someone would try to climb up the outside of the armor, whereupon a shot would ring out from a trailing vehicle and, like a flea picked cleanly off the dog, would slink to the ground and be trampled underfoot by the crowd.

The vehicles slowed a few times, and when they did, the crowds would clench around them, forcing the convoy to push forward again, clearing abandoned and crippled cars in their path by pushing them to the side as they advanced. This give-and-take uncertainty caused the mass of crowd and metal to be intermingled, and sometimes when the convoy picked up steam it would lurch quickly and run over something, *or someone,* lying in the road.

Heedless, or perhaps spellbound and in shock, other refugees along the highway kept up their march, heads bowed and gathered tightly in packs, their children huddled in the midst of them. These people didn't even look up to notice the bodies of the dead and the dying. Screams broke through the cold air like glass breaking, but the packs of humans huddled even more closely together, shuffling like zombies into the coming night.

The trio sat under the cover of trees and watched the scene in its horrifying extremity. Lang looked down and wondered how they would ever get across the highway. It is odd where minds go for answers in such moments. Lang unsnapped his backpack and lowered it slowly to the ground. He wondered for a moment if there was anything in Clay's bag that would provide them a solution, or perhaps comfort, in the present situation. *Maybe Walt Whitman, or Hemingway, or C.L. Richter had some advice for crossing through a warzone highway... for passing through death,* he thought.

*Probably not...*

From Walt Whitman:

*Allons! through struggles and wars!*
*The goal that was named cannot be countermanded.*

*Have the past struggles succeeded?*
*What has succeeded? yourself? your nation? Nature?*
*Now understand me well- it is provided in the essence of things that*
*from any fruition of success, no matter what, shall come forth something to make a greater struggle necessary.*

*My call is the call of battle, I nourish active rebellion,*
*He going with me must go well arm'd,*
*He going with me goes often with spare diet, poverty, angry enemies,*
*desertions.*

*Allons! the road is before us!*
*It is safe- I have tried it- my own feet have tried it well- be not detain'd!*

# Chapter 3
# Rubicon

Prophecy is a funny thing, but not for the reasons one usually assumes. Of course, there is the humorous aspect of it in the common mind, with its messengers in sackcloth, pulling the twigs out of their beards as they stand before the people like some mad messengers of doom. That is funny as far as it goes. And it is funny that no prophet is welcomed in his homeland. It would seem that the people should be more likely to accept the word of someone they know rather than someone they don't, perhaps especially so if they knew the courage required to stand up and warn one's neighbors. However, this is distinctly *not true* with prophets. The people would rather they go warn somebody else and leave them be with their pesky opinions.

No. All of that is true, but none of it is the reason that prophecy is funny. Rather, it is funny because prophecy often tells us one thing, but we distinctly hear something else. It is as if God in heaven decided to give us a message, and chose to do it through one of our fellows. Somewhere along the line, the message is garbled, like in those games we played as children where we sat in a circle and passed some sentence around, so that the last person heard something totally different from the original intended message. Couldn't God, if he were inclined to give us a message, find a more suitable way than to pass it through gossip? Couldn't the people be saved from their vices if they were simply inclined to listen a little better, perhaps to see with their own eyes?

*Of course, not.* Because prophecy, by definition, is pointing to something that hasn't happened yet. And we, in our moment, only see what affects us in our immediate space. Everything that hasn't happened yet *to us* is speculative in our eyes.

That was the case with Lang as he sat as still as he possibly could, pressing his head against the stone wall, feeling its cold against his temple. His memory suddenly flashed to a prophecy given by his hero, the great writer Alexander Solzhenitsyn. *"The next war..."* Solzhenitsyn said, *"may well bury Western civilization forever."* That should have suggested to him the larger picture of the wider world. It should have made him remember the long talks with Volkhov in which the old man had told him of impending worldwide calamity.

Instead, as he sat nursing his bullet wound, trying not to cry out in pain, all he could think of was how "western civilization" had come, in his own mind at that moment, to equate with him—*just him*. That somehow he was the entire focus and culmination of history. Being wounded, and living through it, had a way of drawing a man inward, and as he sucked in his breath and felt the tug as Peter stanched the blood, he wondered whether the war that was around him would bury him like it seemed to be burying western civilization.

\* \* \* \*

The crossing of Highway 17 hadn't gone smoothly. They'd decided from their vantage point at the treeline overlooking the road that they would move as silently as possible up the highway access road, camouflaged within the thick stands of trees that pushed up against the clearing. They were looking for a better place to cross. Peter explained that they wanted to make their move sometime after dark, and they looked for a place where the clearing between the trees narrowed and the crowd thinned somewhat.

They found one, a place where the road was somewhat more destitute of refugees and obstructions. Most of the traffic had stopped for the night, and they walked a mile up the highway, toward the north. The road there turned straight westward and took a short dip to the south, and they found a little bend in the highway that they determined would be the best place for them to attempt a crossing.

As darkness descended like a curtain on the area, the three halted their plodding through the trees, hid among the bushes, and surveyed the scene before them.

The refugees on the highway huddled in small groups and started large bonfires from anything they could find that would burn in order to stay warm. While there was scattered violence here and there, the people down below them seemed to be intent on hunkering down for the cold night on the highway and its easement for some reason devoid of any appreciable logic. Misery loves company, but less often is it recognized that company, especially the wrong kind, often *invites* misery. As the three looked down on the scene, they saw that there was less company here perhaps, and therefore less attendant misery, so they determined that it was here that they would take their shot.

Peter spotted a place where there was at least a football field's distance between campfires, and he pointed out quietly to Lang and Natasha that there were no campfires burning in the woods in the distance across the wide expanse of roadway and greenbelt. "This is where we cross," he said, as they looked down on the stygian scene.

The plan was to sprint the distance in irregular intervals so that they would not *all* get caught out in the open at the same time. Looking out across the distance, they determined the shortest route and marked a reference point to run towards, and they decided that Peter would go first. He would carry both his own bag and Natasha's. "If something happens to me, God forbid, if I stumble or fall, I'll throw the bags as far from my body toward the opposite side as I can, and you must try to gather them in on a sprint as you make your own way across." Lang thought of stories that Volkhov had told him of the storming of the beaches at Normandy. The soldiers, when taking heavy fire from the enemy, had tossed their guns up the beach so that, if the worst happened, the soldiers who actually made it farther up the sand would have more firepower ahead of them in their fight.

"Don't look back, or to the side. Just put your head down and run," Peter said as he touched them each on the shoulder. With that, he gathered his breath in and turned to run.

Lang and Natasha watched his burly figure push out across the snow and then gather speed when he reached the road, keeping low to the ground. In a normal circumstance, Peter's movements would have appeared clumsy and bulky as he sprinted like a bear across the clearing with the two bags heaving on his back. Perhaps from the perspective of anyone who might have seen him, he did appear to be a bear, but in any event, he made it safely across without even raising a protest from the distance, and he disappeared into the woods beyond. Lang was shocked. *Maybe this is going to be easier than we thought*, he tried to encourage himself.

Once on the other side, Peter made his way into the trees and found a safe place to stow the bags, and, returning to the tree line, he stood poised to watch the others cross, to be ready in case they needed help.

Natasha crossed next, and she did well enough, though one of the parties surrounding a campfire spotted her and a shout of "Hey! Over there!" rang out through the night. Peter was on alert to see if she was going to be chased or followed, but she wasn't, so before long, panting and out of breath, she joined Peter in the trees on the south side of the highway.

There was a stirring in one of the camps, so Lang waited several more minutes. When no one came out searching, or ventured over near the wire where the two had crossed back into the woods, he decided it was safe to make his own venture across the Rubicon. He thought of old black and white films of East Germans sprinting for freedom before a shot would ring out, and their bodies would tumble headlong into the razor wire. *That ought to keep me running*, he thought, and he reached down with a stick and cleared the snow from the soles of his boots.

Lang made his start, and, almost from the beginning, Peter could see that the attempt was not going to go well. Lang tripped at the starting gate and fell, sprawling into the snow on the upwards low climb to the main highway, and Peter, from his vantage point, noticed that some men to his left, who had reacted to Natasha's dash across the roadway, were gathering and pointing toward the shadow he made on the snow. They began to approach the area at the top of the incline where Lang was struggling to regain his footing. Peter watched as Lang regrouped and began his run in earnest.

27

The men broke into a jog toward him as he crested the low hill, and Peter saw that they had an angle on him, so that they would almost certainly cut him off before he could make it to safety. He watched as the men converged on Lang's path and anticipated whether he would have to run to his aid.

Feinting to the left, Lang made it past the first defender, before a second man who made it into the middle distance between Lang and the trees cut him off. Angry shouts rang out and someone yelled, "Hey, give me that bag!"

Lang picked up his speed, finding traction now as the adrenaline rush made his body surge forward. Another of the assailants was sprinting toward him trying to stop him in his tracks, but Lang swerved and pivoted in the other direction. He had spent his life fleeing bullies, and now that lifetime of training kicked in. He maneuvered across the field at an angle, determined not to let these untrained hooligans do what the professional bullies he'd faced in Warwick could not.

Sprinting now at full-speed he almost casually and effortlessly detached his backpack's waist band, and, grabbing the padded arm strap in a single fluid motion, he swung it's full weight at his nearing attacker, juking to his right again simultaneously. The bag caught the man flush in the side of the head, and the bully tumbled to the ground, yelping in pain. This action caused a cacophonous cry of protest from the other men who were approaching from the rear, slow and lumbering, unable to get any traction in the ice and snow. Lang bent over, scooped up his bag, and ran toward the trees.

In the flickering night, he suddenly sensed a smooth air of calm as he warmed with the excitement and accomplishment of his escape. He noticed his shadow on the ground, running before him, as cast by the moon over his shoulder. He thought it beautiful and sublime, the motion of its lengthening stride, the way its feet met his own as it sprinted toward safety in front of him.

Just as suddenly as he had come to appreciate the pleasure of his own shadow—his own running—he came to question what became of it. In that expanded microsecond he heard a calamitous noise in the distance, and it sounded like an explosion over his shoulder, and he looked down at his shadow and saw the red splotches on its torso. He spun around in a jerking, involuntary motion like someone had run over him with a car, but he turned his head to watch his shadow until the last moment, and then he slammed to the ground whereupon the shadow disappeared.

Now, he was only Vasily Kashporov lying on the cold hard ground in the snow, with a bullet wound in his shoulder.

\* \* \* \*

Lang knew that something had struck him but did not know what it was and he felt no pain. He had to get up, and as he did the thought crossed his mind that he was already free. He didn't know at the time *why* that particular thought crossed his mind, but he did know that he was no longer helpless little Vasily, cowering from bullies. He was now a free man, and had tasted freedom, and he liked it. Solzhenitsyn said, "You only have power over people so long as you don't take everything away from them. But when you've robbed a man of everything, he's no longer in your power—he's free again." Lang had suddenly come face to face with his death, and he determined that he would get up and run, and somehow this made him feel whole again. He liked being free, and he ran like the wind.

Almost instantaneously upon hearing the shot and seeing Lang tumble to the ground, Peter had vaulted out of the trees and, operating on adrenaline of his own, he was sprinting towards Lang like an Olympian. The younger man had regained his feet and was rapidly continuing his progress. Peter met him and grabbed him firmly, hurrying him along, and the two friends made it back into the trees before the men in the distance could decide just what they'd seen.

The assailants stopped, tired and out of shape, and they did not follow their victim into the woods. If they had been asked what stopped their pursuit, they would have sworn up and down that they had just seen a bear run out of the woods to save a man.

* * * *

Most Americans, prior to the events that were now unfolding in their country, would have denied that such random acts of violence and wanton cowardice would have been possible, but that is because most Americans are insulated from reality. Woefully so. They are ignorant of world history and the conditions of life experienced through most of the last millennia by much of the rest of the world. When people have lived their lives carelessly, in the lap of comforts and the bosom of excess purchased for them by the hard work and sacrifice of their ancestors; when they have counted on laws and government alone to keep them safe, they come to believe that the same kindnesses they have experienced at the hands of their neighbors heretofore will be granted them when that world collapses. They believe that humanity will not revert to his animal nature when there is a disintegration of those laws, and when the power and ability of that government to impose and keep those laws is not just diminished, but eliminated. In this, they are wrong.

Man, loosed from the bonds of all law, and religion, and conscience, even if those restraints have been false or damaged to begin with, reverts to the animal nature that animates him. It is inevitable, then, that masses of men, loosed from restraints and deprived of access to the artificial means of provision they have counted on for all their lives, will soon experience unprecedented violence and mayhem.

Even if it begins in small places, a little leaven will be enough to leaven the whole lump, and eventually social feelings will collapse along with society. We don't have to like hearing it, but the truth has a way of not caring whether we like it or not.

The world is a violent place when restraints are removed. The already vanishing traditions of human care and kindness, peacefulness, and lawful living have been systematically eradicated by dialecticians who maintain power by championing division and by pitting neighbor against neighbor, race against race, and party against party. The bloody product of this will seem barbarous and horrible to those who have yet to experience it. This is strong medicine. But in times of sickness, it is medicine that is needed.

# Chapter 4
# Good Medicine

Peter checked to see if anyone was following them. No one was. Tracking quickly through a low gully and into the deeper woods, after a good five-minute walk, they came upon a stone fence line in the snow separating a field from the surrounding forest. He pulled Lang down into the snow and, by touch and instinct more than sight, he felt for the wound that he knew to be in Lang's left arm or shoulder. He needed to know how serious it was before he made any decisions about what to do next. He found it, the wound, and it seemed to be a minor one in the larger scheme of things, with a clear entry and exit in the fat of the tissue. Lang was blessed that the bullet had not struck any bone, and the young man was working on adrenaline and seemed to be unconcerned by the fact that he had just been shot. In fact, he was slightly delirious.

"You've been shot, Lang." Peter said. "But I don't think it is too serious. A scratch, really."

"Wow," Lang replied, his right hand reaching upwards to feel the wound. He drew back his hand with blood on it, and he grimaced slightly, but not from the pain. "I've never been shot before."

"Well, now you're an expert," Peter said, cupping his hand behind the young man's neck. "I think you'll be okay. We'll move on so that we can put some distance between us and that madness, and then I'll see if we can build camp and clean and dress the wound." He looked at Lang and gave him a smile, then a wink.

"Thank you, Peter." Lang looked back at him with sincere appreciation in his eyes.

"No problem, son," Peter said, his smile perhaps grimmer than he had hoped. "Now let's move out."

The way was dark and they moved very slowly, mostly by feel. Natasha switched bags with Lang so she could carry the heavier of the loads and take some of the weight off his shoulders as he slowly began to come back into his body. There was just enough moonlight to allow them to see from tree to tree and make their way, as if by braille, through the low valley. The branches clung like webs to the nighttime sky, and the brush caught their clothes as they swept past.

These valleys, cut by receding glacial ice, ran primarily from northeast to southwest, which was good for the Warwickians as they made their escape. It meant that they could move steadily through the darkness without having to do a lot of climbing and descending.

Peter intended to walk for a good thirty minutes, but their pace, though steady, was so slow that it was nearly two hours before he felt that they had put enough distance between themselves and the road. They walked a little further, and then the trio came upon a low stone building, very small—

maybe eight feet by eight feet. Peter identified it as an old well house.

The building had a wooden door that had mostly rotted away, and around the top of the building, where there had once been a few small windows, were now jagged slices of glass, long ago smashed and broken by who knows what or whom. It took the three of them a good fifteen minutes to drag out all of the trash that had accumulated in the building over the years, but before long, they had it cleaned out enough to use for the night. The floor of the well house was cement, and in the center of the building was only a protruding water pipe, maybe six inches in diameter, which someone had covered with a large rock.

Peter built a very small fire inside the building and explained that he would only let it burn as long as necessary. Fire is a beacon, but sometimes it is necessary, so he intended to obscure it from view as best as he could. He needed to produce coals that they could use to cook their food and heat water for cleaning Lang's wounds, and then he would let the fire burn just long enough to heat the stones of the building itself, for heat in the night, before the fire would be extinguished.

The big man prepared and started the small fire and showed Natasha how to feed wood into it without letting the flame get too big, and then he took the gun and told Lang he would patrol the perimeter and keep watch until they had enough glowing red coals to do what they needed to do. He stepped out into the night to have a look around.

Lang and Natasha sat for a moment, and she tended the fire and watched him in silence.

"Are you holding up?" he asked, seeing her sink deeper into thought.

"Yes," Natasha sighed. "I'm fine. I'm just worried about you... and thinking about Kolya."

"I know," Lang said. "I am sorry Cole didn't make it back in time." He noticed as she looked up in distress at the mention of that name, with a silent insistence that he call her brother by his given name. "Natasha, I'm going to keep calling him Cole because I believe him still to be alive. I'm sure he is okay. He is a resourceful fellow."

"Oh, there is no need to lie, Lang. We both know that he would not have disappeared unless something bad had happened to him. He probably fell into some criminals' hands and now he's—"

"Stop. Don't think that way. He's fine." Lang looked at her and wished that he could be more certain of that fact, but the remembrance of the bombed-out remains of Warwick flashed through his mind. The simple truth was that nothing was fine. He shifted his back against the wall and suddenly felt a pain shoot down through his arm and realized that, even on that account, there was nothing about the situation that was fine.

"Here. Let me take a look at you," Natasha said, and she pulled Lang's shirt back slightly, hearing the cold sucking sound of the coagulated blood ripping slightly from his skin as she bent over his wound.

"Ow, Ow. Ow!" Lang said, before he gritted his teeth and leaned back again into the wall, suddenly becoming aware of the warmth in her hands.

"Is it bad?"

"It's fine. It'll be okay."

"Now who's lying?" Lang replied, attempting a small grin as a kind of gallows humor. Natasha grinned back, and somehow this made the pain in his arm begin to lessen.

They sat and talked as Natasha tended to the fire, and they both tried to encourage each other for what seemed like an hour. They spoke of the strangeness of their journey and the tiredness of their hopes. They talked of how their lives had seemed somehow... shortened... having been ripped out from under them by the flash of recent events. "It seems like yesterday that Kolya and I were getting ready for the Fall Festival," Natasha said.

"It seems like a minute ago that you were telling him to stop with his damned Shakespeare," Lang smiled. "I wonder what he would have to say about this fine mess..."

In that vein, they went on speaking and reminiscing, echoing the same kind of conversation that was taking place around millions of campfires at that very moment, spread across the landscape of America and, beyond that, the globe.

Indeed, had one been lodged in the middle distance between heaven and earth at that moment; or maybe parachuting down from the outer reaches of space in a tumbling freefall that had not yet leveled out; had one not gained a controlling vantage point in that middle distance; if one had looked upward and then downward in that tumbling spiral in the darkness of space, it would have been difficult to tell which were the fires burning on the ground around the millions of campfires like this one, and which ones were raging in the hearts of a million stars.

\* \* \* \*

Before long, Peter returned from his patrol, and, seeing that the fire was prepared and ready, he used a piece of scrap corrugated tin from the refuse pile to scoop hot coals into two shallow holes dug just outside the building. Each of the holes was about five inches deep and just big enough around to receive the stainless steel pans from the mess kit in his pack.

He built up the fire in the building by adding more of the old two-by-fours and scraps of wood from the refuse pile, and then he closed the dilapidated door to obscure the fire, as much as possible, from anyone who might be lurking in the shadows of the woods. They would let the inside fire burn for an hour, and then they would sweep it out and douse it with the snow. The old stones of the building would then emit their warmth throughout the night as the three friends slept like buns in an old stone oven. At least, that was the theory.

Lang and Natasha watched as Peter filled one of the pots with snow to melt for boiling, and in the other, he placed some food from the backpacks to warm. He watched diligently over both pots and continued to add snow to the water pan as it melted down. Lang noticed that it took a lot of snow to create an appreciable amount of water. Once that pan was full and boiling, he placed two ripped cloths from his pack into the water and let them boil for several minutes, and while they boiled, he examined Lang's wound.

"It looks like you were hit with a .22 or a .38. Something small. There is no bullet in the wound, and it is bleeding, but not too profusely. As the bullet passed through, it ripped the skin and flesh, but it doesn't look like it pierced the muscle too deeply." He was silent for a moment as he worked, then he turned to Natasha, who seemed to be terribly worried and afraid. "No arteries were hit, and the bleeding is steady, but not heavy." She nodded her head but kept her hand covering her mouth, as if she might need it there to stifle a cry or sob. "Natasha, dear, could you bring me that bottle of vodka from my pack?"

"Sure," she replied and hustled off to get it, happy again to be of some use. She made a point as she went through the pack to catalog in her mind all of the things she was seeing. She wanted to be able to do this if ever the situation, God forbid, were to arise again.

Returning with the clear bottle of alcohol, she asked, "Are you going to sterilize the wound with it, or give it to him as an anesthetic?"

"Neither, Natasha," he said as he twisted open the bottle and chugged a significant amount. He wiped his mouth with his sleeve, smiled, and then took another long swig before twisting the top back onto the bottle. "I'd give him some as an anesthetic if I were doing major surgery or amputating the limb, just to get him to lie as still as possible, but we're trying to get the bleeding stopped, and alcohol can thin the blood, making it harder to accomplish that. The vodka was for me, to steady my hands and give me strength, because Lang," he said, now looking Lang straight in the eye but with an encouraging smile on his face, "this is going to hurt you *way* more than it's going to hurt me."

Peter extracted one of the cloths from the water with the knife from Lang's pack, and, when it had cooled only a little, he balled up the cloth and applied heavy and direct pressure with the sterilized rag directly on the wound for five full minutes. This was a bigger chore than it seemed, and Lang grimaced from the pain but found the pressure to be soothing in a way that seemed contradictory to him.

After the five minutes was up, Peter released the pressure and gave the wound another five minutes to bleed a little so that he didn't rob the whole arm of necessary blood and oxygen. He then reapplied the pressure with the second rag and returned the first one to the boiling water. The five minutes of pressure seemed like a short time to Natasha, but on the spot and under stress, it seemed like a lifetime to Peter and Lang. She was surprised when Peter removed the pressure this time, and the bleeding had slowed to just a faint trickle.

Natasha viewed the whole scene with amazement, and she was impressed with both Peter's skill, and Lang's bravery and calm during the procedure. She watched as the older man went through his pack, pulled out the first aid kit, and withdrew some tweezers and a scalpel and scissors. He sterilized the medical tools from the first aid kit in the boiling water, and when he was ready, he turned to Natasha and said, "Lang did well with the last step, daughter, but we'll see how *manly* he is now!"

Lang grimaced at that, turned the wince into a weak smile, then closed his eyes, and rolled his head back until the back of it pressed against the stone building.

Peter had Natasha hold the flashlight from Lang's bag, and then he carefully and cautiously removed the dead skin and dying flesh with the scalpel and scissors until he was reasonably certain that the wound was clean and ready to bind up. He then packed the wound with sterile gauze bandages, wrapped it loosely with more gauze from a roll, and then secured it all with medical tape. "You want to keep it fairly loose," he said. "We definitely don't want to cut off the blood supply. A wound needs oxygen, blood flow, and as sterile an environment as possible without infection in order to heal."

"Shouldn't we sew it closed or cauterize it?" Natasha asked.

"No. That's almost never a good idea when in the field, at least in my limited and unprofessional opinion. I would only cauterize it if we were on the run and either Lang, or the limb, was probably not going to make it otherwise. That process is really only for sealing veins or arteries when you don't have time to actually work carefully on the wound. And when you sew it closed, you sew in infection and dead tissue that we probably missed. Since it doesn't have a way to exit, the wound can then get infected. Better to leave it open and let the body heal itself. There'll probably be fluid and pus discharge, and we want that. That's the body's way of cleansing and healing the wound. We'll just keep an eye on it and change the dressing when we can. And listen, Natasha," Peter saw her trying to catalogue all the steps in her mind, and wanted to help her understand, "there are as many opinions about ditch medical care as there are people who have to do it. Always keep your eyes and ears open. Learn and listen. I'm not a doctor or even a paramedic. I've had a few lessons through the years, and I'm just doing what I know. You can always learn to do things better."

Natasha nodded her head. "What about antibiotics?" she asked.

"Uncle Lev had some Cephalexin and Doxycycline in that first aid kit. Grab the Cephalexin and bring me the equivalent of 500 milligrams. If they are 250 milligram pills, then bring me two."

"They are 500 milligram capsules, Peter," Natasha said, bringing the whole bottle to him.

"Just give me one then. We'll give him two a day for a week and hopefully that will knock out any infection."

Peter gave the pill to Lang with some water from a water bottle to wash it down. "That's one of the good things about Warwick..." he paused, not really wanting to say anything good about the town. "Anyway, that was *one* good thing. We didn't have to have prescriptions from a doctor to get first aid medications that are non-addictive. In America, they have to outlaw anyone treating themselves because the medical system and pharmaceutical businesses *were* a lynchpin in the whole economic system. That little bit of corruption was just another finger in the dike of western civilization. The socialists looked at the system and said, 'See! We're keeping

41

the economy afloat!' but look around now and see what their logic has given us. You can float a house on a balloon, but it will pop, and when it does... ahhh, such is the ruin of that house!"

Peter looked at them, to see if they were following his argument. Both of his younger companions seemed more concerned about Lang's pain and discomfort than his argument. They were unaware that he was trying, precisely, to draw their minds *away* from the injury by diverting their attention elsewhere. "Ahh, children," he smiled. "I didn't tell you I was also a Doctor of Philosophy, did I?" He looked at them and pulled a long face, clowning like a parent does with a child who has scraped a knee, until the two youths finally gave in to his merrymaking.

Lang, who had been stoic and brave throughout his treatment, was the first to smile, even though the process of removing the dead and damaged flesh was to the very limit of what he thought he could handle. He thought about what it would be like to be in one of the gulags during a Siberian winter. It's strange what the mind locks onto in such moments. He looked at Peter and told him with his eyes that this experience had not been bad at all.

When Peter was done, Lang thanked him for the work. Peter looked at him and said, "Tonight is probably going to be tough for you, little son. You probably won't sleep because the wound will swell a lot and throb. The shock of the run and the adrenaline from your close escape will wear off, and then the pain will set in. Tomorrow it will hurt a lot, but less so than tonight. If, by tomorrow night, the bleeding has stopped and it looks like healing has begun," he paused, and winked, "I'll get you loaded on the vodka so you can have some relief from the pain and get some sleep."

"Well, I don't think I'll need that!" Lang said, laughing.

"That's what you say now. But tomorrow will be a different story. And if not, then... more for me." With that, Peter took another swig from the bottle before stowing it away in his bag.

# Chapter 5
# War

When she awoke in the morning, Veronica D'Arcy sat bolt upright from her sleeping bag on the hard, flat floor and felt around in the dark for her son.

"Stephen!"

Her voice echoed through the smallish chamber and disappeared into a darkened door leading down a narrow concrete corridor. She peered into the darkness, feeling her son's empty sleeping bag beside her, and called out again, this time with rising emphasis.

"Boy?!"

"Mom?"

The answer came back, a little muffled, from deep in the dark. As Veronica's eyes came into focus, she saw the faint light of a candle playing in shadows at the end of the small, cramped passageway, and that light suddenly turned the corner, throwing a dull orange glow on the walls of either side of the hallway as her son stepped out into the corridor. She saw the glow of the candle illuminate her son's face, his hands leaning the candle forward slightly so the wax would drip on the floor. The flame wicked up in sharp little whiskers, and she could see his wide smile in its effulgence. She watched as he proceeded toward her down the hall and into the chamber. She let her breath out in one long sigh... then remembered where they were and how they'd arrived there.

"Mom? Did you know that there are boxes of stored food back there, and water? There's even a box of contamination gear. And some bikes! There are probably ten or so... I thought you told me this place was abandoned."

"It is. This was a nuclear bunker once upon a time, boy. It was discovered years ago, but that stuff should have been taken out. It's got to be fifty years old by now."

"No. That's what I'm telling you... It's dated 2011. Those boxes are new."

Veronica looked at him, to see if he was pulling her leg. He was a sweet boy, but he had his father's penchant for practical jokes. She looked into his eyes to see if this was one of them. They were the eyes of her John—strong and sparkling—always with a little mirth. But now they just looked hurt, disappointed that she would doubt him. In this moment of all moments, he wanted her to know that he understood the gravity of their situation and why they had dropped everything when the lights went out; why they had fled through the city to this bunker and slipped in under the cover of darkness. He did not, of course, *fully* understand. But he wanted her to know that he was trying.

"Mom... I'm telling you. This place has been prepared for something *now*. There are supplies back there that someone just brought in. It looks like someone means to use this place."

Veronica reached in her bag and felt for her flashlight. It wasn't that she didn't trust her son, but she was interested to see for herself. If someone had prepared the place, that meant that someone might be on the way, and that fact could change her plan, even as she made that plan up on the fly. As she searched her bag, she gently checked her pistol, running her finger over the safety to make sure that she had firmly locked it in place.

"Well, let's have a look then, Stephen," she said, getting up creakily from the floor, her joints aching slightly from sleeping on the cold, hard concrete through the night. She switched on the flashlight and Stephen led her down the hall, the mix of candlelight and flashbulb throwing varying shadows on the walls as they bent over and crept down the hallway to the end of the corridor.

They entered a small stone storeroom and Veronica was amazed to find it exactly as Stephen had described it. There were boxes of recently stored food and water, and ammunition and nuclear fallout gear, bicycles, some medical kits, a couple of lead-lined containers with batteries and walkie-talkies. The find both thrilled and alarmed Veronica, as it presented a tempting cache of items they could use for their survival, but also suggested that they might not be alone for very long. She would have to make a decision. Should they hunker down and hope for the best, or should they grab what they could and make a run for it? Where would they go? What would happen if they left too soon, or too late? These were the questions that swirled through her mind and mixed with the need to tell Stephen, who was smiling and eager beside her, something—anything—to let him know what she suspected might be coming.

"Okay, boy, now we have to think about what we will do." She looked at the beautiful face that, for the last several years, had slowly been approaching the height of her own, perched upon an awkward teenaged body filling out with sinewy muscularity. She took his face in her hands and kissed his forehead. "We have to decide in the face of uncertainty what we are going to do so we can face this world down... wash our feet before we get in de dance." Stephen's face looked back, not comprehending, but ready to follow where she led. Then he smiled.

"Cool, mom. But first, can we have a little breakfast?"

Veronica laughed at her son's bright humor. *There's that playfulness... even in the face of this calamity*, she thought. She pulled a small box marked "Energy Bars" off the top of the pile, and pulled out a small penknife from her pocket and opened the tape. They began to sift through the box and catalogue its contents when, suddenly, they heard a scuffling down the hall.

At first, it sounded like the sound of their hands in the box, crinkling and sifting, echoing across the concrete. Veronica even thought that it *was* their hands for a moment, so she grabbed Stephen's in hers and forced them to be still for a moment so she could listen closely. There. It was distinct now. There was a shuffling of boots across concrete, the noise muffled by the thick steel doors. There was the sound of an argument, bodies pushing and pulling against each other, and then, as certainly the sound began, it ended.

They stood in silence. Veronica wished she had taken her gun from her bag and put it in her waistband. She turned to go back to the front of the bunker and retrieve it when suddenly she heard a barbaric yawp, a bloodcurdling cry from outside the entryway, and what sounded like several bodies came crashing against the outside of the door.

Someone was trying to get in.

\*\*\*\*

## Saturday

Despite what Peter told him, Lang fell asleep easily, passing out from sheer mental and physical exhaustion. He slept through the night, even though the ground made his sleep restless and unsatisfying. The building was warmer than he had supposed it would be, and, for most of the night, the warmth from the earlier fire radiated from the stone floor and walls, and he appreciated that warmth. He even dreamed... in a fit of restless half-waking as the morning neared.

When he was fully awake, he realized that Peter had not come to bed, but had stood watch all through the night. Lang noted that the older man was doing everything he could possibly do to keep him and Natasha safe. He wondered whether, in Peter's mind, because he'd been denied the presence and care of a real family of his own for most of his adult life, he'd adopted the two Warwickian youth as his children. He had now called Natasha "daughter" once and Lang "son" twice. He'd called them his "children." This had happened naturally, but with a hint of reserve, as though Peter hadn't thought about it when he'd done it, but didn't want it to be commented upon now that it was done. This did not bother Lang at all.

It was evident that Peter had embraced their situation, and Lang noticed how the older man now seemed comfortable in his skin, as though his natural skills and human feelings at last had an outlet. After the initial blunt and angry outburst while they were looking out at the wreckage of Warwick from that hill in the distance, Peter had settled into this newfound father figure role admirably. He'd treated both Lang and Natasha tenderly, and he seemed to relish the responsibility he felt for both of them. This gave Lang a twinge of emotion he had not expected to feel toward the man, as he came to feel something that echoed his own long lost sorrow at never having a father.

When Peter came by to check on the two that morning, he didn't seem to be tired at all. He claimed to have fallen asleep for several hours leaning against a tree in the darkness, but both Natasha and Lang knew that this was not true. Peter had taken the gun and watched over them all night like a parent watches over his children when he feels they are in harm's way. Somehow, Lang thought, looking at Natasha and seeing that she shared the sentiment without having to speak it, they had to find a way to get Peter some sleep.

Peter built another fire in the building, and again he filled the two holes with coals. This time he boiled water in both pans and then he went through the process of checking and re-dressing Lang's wound. When he pulled the gauze out of the wound, Lang yelled out, and Peter calmed him and told him that the pain was a good sign. He gave Lang a small piece of leather, the sheath of the knife that Clay had once gotten from Veronica, to bite down on.

"That means the wound is healing and the gauze has dried into the wound," Peter said. "Even though it hurts, ripping the wound open is actually good for it." Lang bit down and looked at Peter through bleary eyes. The older man spread his hands as if to indicate that he could not quite explain exactly *how* it was good, but Lang would just have to trust him. Lang leaned his head back against the now cold stone and blinked that he did.

After Peter was finished caring for the bullet wound, they boiled enough water to fill all of their water bottles, and then, after packing up their gear, by around 8 a.m. they were ready to continue their walk. Checking the map and the compass, Peter plotted a course for them, and they set out through the snow, feeling the weight and mileage in their legs from the previous day's trek.

They continued their southwesterly advance, and they were surprised and pleased to discover that, for most of the day, they moved through empty forestland and not suburban tracts or areas thick with farms and their fences. They made good time, and kept up their cautious movement, advancing steadily until the day began to morph into evening.

As the darkness began to fall, they saw from a low hill a space in the distance where the forest seemed to end, and they noticed the long black shadows of some type of structures that rose above the trees. They couldn't quite make them out at first, but in a moment they could see them, distinct in their regularly placed intervals and structurally different from the chaotic mass of limbs reaching like tentacles into the nighttime sky. They looked like dinosaurs against the darkening heavens, sitting up on a ridge where their skeletons towered over the valley.

As they grew closer, the structures disappeared into the mishmash of branches and darkness immediately over their heads, and they began to hear the now familiar sounds of people and gunfire, first in the distance, and eventually in the foreground. They slowed their approach and wove through the trees, staying hidden among the trunks and the brush until they eventually stepped into a clearing and saw spread out before them what looked, for everything in the world, like a battlefield.

The clearing was now deserted. However, this had only happened recently, because the fires of the encampment of a large group of families were spread here and there throughout the long, clear-cut strip, and the fires still burned.

"As they surveyed the damage and looked around for any signs of movement they heard a crackling overhead and one of the wooden dinosaur looking structures, burning at its base from a fire set near a group of tents around the foundation, came suddenly to groan and creak and then to give way. It crashed to the ground in a huge, roaring din, its tail, connecting it to the other structures, tightening from the weight of the fallen beast before the tension was too much. The fall of the dinosaur and the tension in its tail caused it to snap and whip back upwards, sending a high-pitched ricochet through the valley that made the hikers flinch and step back as the noise whistled down the valley.

\* \* \* \*

The trees and forest ended abruptly in a straight, ruled line and there was a long clearing, and when the three travelers examined the scene they noted that the strip was actually a long beltway that ran from northwest to southeast. Down this long, cleared strip ran power lines, held aloft by enormous wooden towers. The streak of land cut through the forest like a landing strip, and the scene looked, if they hadn't known better, as if planes had merely skimmed in low to the ground and strafed the dozens of encampments along the strip with gunfire. Obviously, the refugees had been using the stretch of clearing as a highway to move from wherever they were to wherever they were going, and, not unlike Highway 17, which was still clear in their minds, this well-traveled route of escape had become a death trap for those who had thought to take the easy way out. In fact, if anything, this strip was the worse for having had one day more for the crowds to indulge in their mayhem.

Peter made sure the trio stayed low, and they moved quickly and with purpose, and they kept their eyes peeled to their surroundings as they surveyed the remains of the battle that had taken place, seemingly just moments before, in the field.

From the destruction, debris, and corpses lying around in the snow, Peter determined that this had been a makeshift refugee camp. He deduced that maybe thirty families had been staying in the clearing until only moments ago. The battle was not long in the past... perhaps an hour or so... but not longer.

The older man knelt down, and his eyes took in the gruesome scene. He looked out into the woods to the south, and he pointed so that Lang and Natasha could follow what he was about to say.

"It looks like they came from that way, through the woods. Some kind of looter raiding party. A gang of thugs, or... maybe they were middle-class teachers, grocers, and lawyers? Who's to know? I'd say it was ten or twelve of them. They came out from the woods. It was not long ago, this very night, because the fires were burning. We heard that noise earlier. It is likely that the refugees had no night vision from staring into the fire. Some of the tents and supplies spilled over into the fires in the confusion. The raiding party probably staked out the place from those trees." He pointed back to the south, along a thicket of brush. "They waited until they felt it was the right time, and then they hit hard and fast. It looks like about two-thirds of the people in this camp didn't even stand a chance, cut down before they could stand up and figure out what was going on. No chance at all to get to any kind of cover." Peter turned and swiveled on his heels as if he were watching the attack in real-time as it played out before him. "The looters took what they wanted, then they went *that* way." He pointed to the northwest, following with his finger up the greenbelt.

Peter didn't want to spend too much time in the refugee camp, but he felt it prudent to do a quick and cursory search for supplies and weapons, anything the looters had missed. Wrapped up inside a fallen tent, they found a .22 Marlin squirrel rifle and about ten boxes of ammunition. Lang was the first to find it, and he silently held it up for Peter to appreciate.

Natasha protested at first, when Peter and Lang took the rifle and packed away the ammunition in Lang's backpack, but Peter explained to her that the people who owned this stuff... they were all gone. And the gun, if left here, would be taken by someone coming by, either by good people with benevolent intentions, or by wicked people with evil intentions. "The only way that we can ensure that it falls into the right hands," he spread his own hands, as if the answer were obvious, "is to take it ourselves. Use it for right purposes."

Despite the clear logic in that argument, Natasha felt conflicted. "You need to know right now," Peter told her, in a firm way, but with concern and kindness, "that much of what we're going to need to survive is going to be found and salvaged from this point forward. We don't have the luxury of hunting down the next of kin, or taking found goods to the sheriff's office or authorities. There are no stores or businesses now... not from what we've already experienced. From what you've seen with your own eyes, Natasha, *there aren't any authorities.*"

Natasha nodded her head, and Peter told her he was glad she understood and that he hoped that she would have the stomach for everything that was ahead of them. "Even if you don't, however, you have to be honest about what we are facing. This is not a movie at the Pushkinsky-Cine. This is our *life* now." She nodded again, and told him that she knew what was required, but that she just didn't want to lose her humanity.

"I am helping you to *save* that humanity, dear daughter," Peter said. He let that sink in for a beat. "We are not in the land of the living anymore."

Peter frowned and she grimaced. Lang bent to pick up his pack. The three of them stood in the clearing for a moment, and the ancient differences between men and women swirled around them as they weighed their thoughts. Unlike the couple from the day before, they silently agreed to let those differences help them rather than tear them apart, and eventually the three of them began to trudge back toward the tree line, making their way out of the clearing.

Just as they were turning to take their leave, however, Natasha told them to stop. The men almost turned to anger. Peter drew in his breath to rebuke Natasha and tell her to get past her doubts. He looked at her as if to warn her that they had to get moving and was just about to speak in his impatience.

It was only then that he heard what she was hearing. Natasha raised her hand as if to quiet him, and he held his breath and followed the signal of her pointing.

A moan came from one of the collapsed tents. They rushed to it and lifted its canvas and dug into its crevices to find the door. Once they had found it, they gently lifted the tent away until they found her.

She was beaten and bruised, and terribly afraid, but she was alive. She was still in the land of the living.

# Chapter 6
# Living Truth

Dostoevsky said that "the best definition of man is: a being that goes on two legs and is ungrateful."

Lang could not help feeling that this was true of himself at that instant, as he realized that the woman in the tent was alive and that her injury was minor and survivable. He did not mean to think of rushing away and abandoning her. Such an act certainly would never have occurred to his conscious mind willingly, but it occurred nonetheless.

Somewhere in his *unconscious* mind, his reckoning of the stench of death and fire in the clearing mixed with his guilt at the thought of leaving, his conscience burned brightly like the flames of perdition. He smelled it like charred goose feathers in his nostrils, and he melted in those flames. Had he so soon forgotten his own relatively recent deliverance from bondage? From injury? Was he that ungrateful? He considered himself a man of human compassion and was he so soon to be devoid of that feeling? His face flushed.

Lang had never really read the Bible much, but he was aware of many of its teachings, and one of the ones he liked most was the notion that a man could show no greater love than to lay down his life for others. He caught himself in his quick brush with self-centeredness and reached down a hand to help the woman off the ground. Maybe only a man who is aware of his weaknesses and failings can properly love in that way.

\* \* \* \*

Elsie was her name and she was barely conscious. It took some doing to carry her into the woods and into some similitude of safety. Lang had a wounded arm, and they dared not drop their packs or weapons, so the going was slow, but they eventually accomplished the task. Once they were in cover among the trees, Peter went to work again with the first aid kit. Before long, he had her forehead wound cleaned up with not too much trouble. It was harder to get her to take the two aspirin that Peter gave her for her headache than it had been to carry her into the woods. It helped Peter that the woman was in shock and that she didn't put up too much of a fight.

Before long, and with some water and attention, Elsie was able to give her name and ask where she was. She began to piece together her new reality. Peter noticed right away that this lady was made of stern stuff.

Elsie knew that her husband was dead. She'd seen as much before she lost consciousness. Even though she'd been struck in the head with a rifle butt at the onset of the attack, she didn't lose consciousness immediately, she told them. Her husband, before being shot to death, and in the midst of the confusion from the raid, was able to hide his injured wife in their tent. She was peeking through the tent flap with her hand over her own mouth to stifle her cries and her overwhelming need to scream, and she'd started to lose consciousness when she saw one of the men shoot her husband in the head. That's when she passed out, and now here she was awake to find out that her nightmare was very real. She looked at her three saviors, and seemed to beg their forgiveness in her eyes if she didn't find it in her to appear more grateful. This reality had only gotten worse for her.

As she told her story, Natasha sat down beside the woman and placed an arm around her waist. She could tell that Elsie wasn't sure what the intentions of these three people were, and she wanted the woman to know that she was in good company now. With the telling of her story done, through sobs and tears, Elsie collapsed into Natasha's arms and the men fell silent with nothing to say that might even begin to help.

Peter and Lang had their guns at the ready, torn between allowing this woman space to grieve for a short moment and the need to get moving before more trouble came through the woods or up the greenbelt.

Elsie's sobs faded, and now she seemed to draw strength from somewhere unknown. She placed hands on her knees and tried to push herself up, falling woozily back into Natasha's arms as Peter reached out to lend a hand.

"We have to bury my husband."

Lang and Peter exhaled in unison, and Peter's jaw tightened as he drew in another breath. He consciously scanned the horizon in every direction for the trouble that he knew was surely coming. The two men stepped to the side to confer, leaving Natasha to comfort Elsie.

Peter and Lang stared into one another's eyes for a moment, recognizing the difficulty of the situation. Neither man said a word for one, two, three seconds... then Lang's eyes softened.

He shrugged and nodded, and Peter's jaw tightened again, but this time the older man closed his eyes and nodded his head in agreement.

"Ma'am," Peter said as gently as he could manage, kneeling down in front of her so his voice would be soft and low. "I am sorry about your husband. I know that doesn't help you, hearing me say that, but it's the truth. The three of us have lost more friends in the past couple of days than you can possibly imagine. None of us is immune to loss... but," he paused and searched for the best words to say what he had to say, "there are some things... I need..." He paused again and took a deep breath.

"Ma'am... we're in the middle of cataclysmic meltdown. The whole country and, really, the whole world as far as we know... it's never going to be the same. I can't explain entirely, but let's just say that I have an uncle, he was a friend to all of us... his name was Lev. He was... well... let's say that he was a highly-placed official. He wasn't really, but that'll help you believe what I have to say. Lev told us that there are probably going to be 300 million people dead or dying in the next year, and... well... frankly..." he hesitated for a moment, looking at her to see if she was willing to believe him, "we can't bury 300 million people.

"All of them are real people, and they all have loved ones, but we just can't do it. Nobody can."

Elsie looked into Peter's eyes without anger or hatred or even confusion. He saw that she believed him, even with his roundabout way of telling her the truth. But then something else flashed in her eyes.

"I'm not asking you to bury 300 million people," she said. "I'm merely asking you to bury my husband."

* * * *

The burial was harder than they could possibly have imagined. The ground, being frozen solid in the north in winter, meant that in the old days, bodies were simply placed in a back, unheated room. Burials happened in the spring when the ground softened and shovels could break it more easily. However, you try telling that to a woman who just saw her husband murdered before her eyes. Tell her that you can't bury the body because the ground is frozen.

Peter looked into her eyes and determined that she was an intelligent woman, and reason would return to her in good time. Nevertheless, for right now, Elsie needed a token that would let her turn her back on her dead husband and walk toward the rest of her life. She needed to have closure, and so Peter needed to find some way to bury the man that would give her that token... but it needed to happen quickly, and they had nothing even approximating the proper tools.

Peter had a mini camp shovel in his pack, and Lang had the knife and a stick. They quickly located and dragged Elsie's husband into the woods. She'd pointed out the area where he had gone down and described what he was wearing, and they had rushed quickly out into the clearing to retrieve him. So quickly in fact, that they had pulled off his shoes while they were dragging him.

Glenn was his name. Peter seemed to be intent on noting that as they collected his body. Lang just noted that he was tired of digging graves.

They set themselves to digging. They couldn't go very deep. To do so would just be impossible with the tools at hand. They scratched down a few inches under the snow, and when they could go no further, they dragged Glenn's body into the indentation and searched around for twenty minutes to find enough rocks so that they could pile them on the body. They ended up with an above ground burial. The rocks would serve—as much as possible—to keep the animals from the corpse. Elsie would just have to understand, because, well, it was winter and the ground was now frozen. They had no tools. What else can you say?

They gathered around the grave with Elsie, and no one said anything. What do you say in such moments, standing at a stranger's grave with a woman you don't know who has just lost her husband? Peter thought of his wife and children. Lang thought of his town and felt the pain shooting through his arm. Natasha thought of her brother.

After a few minutes, Elsie just nodded and walked away. Peter and Lang once again caught one another's eyes as they turned their backs on Glenn and the specter of needless, wanton death. Natasha lingered for just a moment and looked into the night's sky. She saw in a patch of blue-black darkness a line of geese flying overhead through the stillness. She would have sworn that the geese's *Ya-honk* was an accusation, but for the life of her, at that moment, she could not have explained just why.

\* \* \* \*

They picked up their trek to the southwest, and Natasha walked along near Elsie, asking her questions as they passed through the snow. Elsie stayed behind Natasha, and the men were on each flank, stationed ten yards to each side of the women. When the way narrowed, Peter would go first, Lang would bring up the rear, and they had learned to be more diligent and aware, as they were a larger group now and someone spotting them from a distance was more likely. Twice they properly spied out other travelers and were able to hunker down and wait in cover until the walkers passed by. On one of those occasions, five men carrying guns walked through in single file and at close ranks, oblivious to their surroundings, within yards of our four travelers who silently hid in the brush—Peter and Lang with guns at the ready.

Back on the march, they occasionally talked to one another, but only barely above a whisper, while their eyes still scanned the surroundings.

"We were married for 24 years," Elsie told Natasha. "I can't say it was perfect, but what marriage is? It was better than anyone else's that we knew... for most of those years, anyway. I loved Glenn, and I know that he loved me and our children..." Her voice trailed off as she thought about her children. They walked on in silence a few steps, then she continued.

"Two girls and a boy... two women and a man now... they've all moved away. We were all raised to believe that children leaving and going out into the world is the way it's supposed to be, you know? I don't believe that anymore, but that's the way it was. Anyway, they went to college first, and then to distant jobs. The two girls are in New York City, and our boy, Glenn, Jr., he's in Idaho. Boise, we think." Natasha looked at her, as if to ask the question, and Elsie answered before she could. "We don't get to talk to him much. He was *different.*"

"What do you mean 'different'?" Natasha asked.

"He talked about all this... *stuff,*" Elsie said, indicating all around them with her hand. "You know, the stuff that's going on right now. He was a survival nut. I guess you'd call him that. We called him that anyway... you know, in trying to *reason* with him. But he wouldn't be reasoned with. He was always going on about something. Anti-government is what I thought, though he always denied it. He was always predicting the *end of the world*, even though he denied that too. I guess I heard what I wanted to hear... anything that would allow me to reject the things he *actually* said. What he did say was that some bad things were going to happen, and that we should change our lifestyles and be more preparedness minded. I didn't understand it all, but... well..." She let the implications of that hang in the air, still unwilling, entirely, to believe it.

"I'm sorry that you didn't get along," Natasha said.

"We just took everything he said as a rejection of us *personally*, as people, as parents, as Americans... whatever. When someone tells you that your way of living is unsustainable or foolish, it makes you mad as hell, you know? Not in a way that is measurable though, it's more like a burning in you that really gets to you. It makes you want to lash out and defend yourself, your worldview... your... I don't know how to say it. Anyway, I know *now*. I figured this out when I watched your men here bury Glenn. All that anger I felt was not at anything Glenn Jr. ever said. I was angry that what he said made my conscience burn."

Elsie was quiet awhile, thinking as she walked along, and Natasha did not interrupt her thoughts.

"The things I said about my own son, the things I did behind his back... well, they were shameful. I wanted to have a relationship with him, but it was like having this accuser around, looking me in the eye all the time. Even when Junior wasn't around, I felt him accusing me."

Natasha walked, and listened. She reached her hand out to steady Elsie as she became aware that the older woman was breathing hard.

"I mean, he wouldn't do it directly... not directly. He just said these *things*. And he *believed* them. I mean, he'd let other people take them or leave them, but he was so damned sure of himself. He never said, 'you are a bad person' or 'you shouldn't do this or that,' or anything like that. But when he talked about the world and the problems in it, then he was talking about *me*. I took that personally, wouldn't you? I felt it was a personal attack.

"Of course I know that it was not *meant* to be personal. I mean, I know that now. I'm his mother, for goodness sake.

But it hurt our relationship. Things were always tense. Truth be told, I guess I got somewhat personal myself on occasion. I would have preferred that he had fallen into line, tossed out his beliefs and just embraced what all the rest of us believed. That was wrong of me... I see that. And it would have been wrong even if it had turned out that he was wrong and everyone else was right." Elsie's voice trailed off and her thoughts went elsewhere for a moment.

"I would give anything to have him here with us while we are going through all of this."

"Did you say he was in Boise?"

"Yes. He moved up there a few years ago. There are many survivalist-minded types up there. I called them worse things before all this happened, but I won't do that now. He tried to get us to come and check out his place, but we wouldn't do it. We thought he was crazy."

"Well, just because he was right about the world, doesn't mean he wasn't crazy!" Natasha said, trying to lighten Elsie's mood.

"He wasn't crazy," Elsie replied flatly.

\* \* \* \*

"We left Binghamton the day after the power went out. They told me it was an 'EMP', but I still don't really know what that means. The stores were soon out of food... it only took *four hours* and they were stripped bare. My son used to rail on about that. I remember it now because I hated hearing it.

"He would say, 'People are crazy if they really believe that the food in the system will last three days after a big enough collapse!' I just wanted him to shut up about it. But he was right. We went into some stores and there were fistfights over the stupidest things. On one aisle, the only things hanging on the wall were some of those gel soles things... you know... the gel-filled pads you cut and put into your shoes to make them more comfortable? Anyway, people were actually fighting over those. Actually fist-fighting over them. Violence! Over some stupid gel soles." Elsie shook her head and Natasha smiled, hearing the incredulity in the woman's humor.

"We just got out of there. All you were going to get in the stores was *killed*."

"That's almost unbelievable. I mean, if we hadn't already seen the things we've seen, I'd call you a liar." Natasha said.

"There's no lying about it. We had almost no food in the house. Not anything to speak of. We usually ate out before this happened." Elsie shook her head. "We made it a few days, but things were getting really thin, and we heard about gangs and looters going door to door. That's when we decided we needed to get out."

"Where were you planning to go?"

"There was no real plan. Some of the neighbors got everyone on our block together and we had a meeting and just decided to get out of the city. That's all we could think of at the time. Just get *out*. You know... get a tent and get out into the country and just forage. It sounded easy. It wasn't. But I suppose you all have gone through the same things?"

"I guess you could say it was something like that," Natasha answered.

"One of the men on our street had a bunch of survival food, and a little hand-pump water purifier, so we figured we'd just walk into the woods until we found some place better than where we were. Isn't that the story of all refugees for all time?"

"I suppose it is."

"So tell me about you all. Who's who?"

Natasha thought for a moment, not knowing what she should say. "Our story is not unlike yours. We're from a town called Warwick."

"Oh, Warwick... I've heard of it," Elsie replied.

"My brother was with me," Natasha said quickly, hoping to cut off any questions in case Elsie knew someone in the other Warwick, or in case she might ask details that would not match up if cross-checked. "He left his glasses at one of our camps and went back for them. We haven't seen him since. I'm very worried."

"Oh, honey! I'm sorry. I'm so sorry. I'm sure he's okay."

"I don't know."

"You probably all should have stuck together, you know. But he'll catch up with you, I'm sure of it."

"I hope you're right," Natasha said, but she didn't believe for a moment that Elsie was right. Natasha rejected the kind of Pollyanna thinking that was common to so many modern Americans. Peter had warned them to beware of it. This one thing was a tiny microcosm of what had caused the dependency, lethargy, and deception in the first place... the tendency to believe that everything would somehow work out okay.

Elsie smiled at her, trying to be comforting. "The sun will come out tomorrow, and he'll be here. You can bet your bottom dollar on that. He's probably just a day behind us. That's all," Elsie said.

This woman, Natasha thought, however good her motives might be, didn't have a single fact on which to base her assessment. She didn't know what had happened to Cole, and an honest judgment, based on the facts on the ground as they had all seen them, did not offer much hope for Cole at all. But discourse in America was about emotions and feelings, and never truth and facts. Natasha had to get used to this reality, because it was a tricky one that could trap you if you weren't careful.

People had the idea that if they were just *positive minded* then nothing bad could happen to them. Or, they thought that if they lied to themselves and one another, then the truth would be easier to swallow later on. Natasha was not going to fall for that, but she appreciated the heart behind the deception.

Herein she could see the clash of worldviews that had multiplied and expanded to bring about this catastrophe, and would continue to cause dissolution if it continued going forward. Beyond the wars and fighting and destruction, there would need to be a reassertion of the age-old desire for truth and honesty. The mind of reason would need to triumph over the generation's long reign of emotionalism and lies. What was it that Lang was always saying? It was a Solzhenitsyn quote that he was fond of repeating...

"One word of truth outweighs the world."

Natasha hoped that somehow, from among the rubble, the truth, and a love of it, would one day rise, stand back up on its feet, and stare the world down again.

# Chapter 7
# Reality

Life can turn on a dime. Sometimes, things are going along as expected and then a vicious pirouette occurs. It's as if we are chasing a beast through the forest and we think we have it right where we want it, and then it turns. It pivots and bares its fangs. In a flash, tables are turned, momentum is lost, victors become vanquished, and lives are lost. In those moments, all we can do is hold on and watch the thing happen.

**Sunday**

The day was crisp and clean, and except for the snow that was still thick on the ground, it might have been spring. It was that bright and airy. The snow crunched under boots, and the reflection of the sun off the snow made the eyes of the four cautious hikers squint into the brightness. After a few hours of good, hard walking, Lang called to Peter and told him that he needed to take a pause. Nature, he explained, was calling. He needed to urinate.

Peter smiled, and in that smile, he let down his guard. He also let down his pack, and so did Natasha. The three hikers with Lang tried to take advantage of the respite by releasing the weight of the backpacks from their backs. They came to rest on the side of a low mountain.

Moments like these can be critical. They can define ultimate success or failure. Perhaps this is unfair, but it is undeniable. These moments represent that one small turn of the screw, or that one nail left undone, that can bring the whole structure down. They are the gaps in eternal vigilance, when people are in moments of peril, and when they ought to remain in a heightened state of awareness. They are that beat of relaxing just a little too much, that tendency to make false assumptions about the situation, or to discount the proximity of danger... well, it is in such moments that mistakes are made. It happens in war and in peace, and it often costs lives.

Peter had already made a few mistakes, but he was not immune to making them again. Nobody is perfect; but imperfection, depending on the situation, can bring about a wide range of consequences... from the inconsiderable to the severe. Peter had only taken a moment, just a small little window, to relax and talk with his travel companions, utilizing Lang's break for a break of his own. But that was all that was required.

Lang walked into a nearby thicket to do his business. He looked into the sky and watched a hawk swoop by, and he felt the relief ease from his bladder. Done, he was beginning to zip his hiking pants when he heard the shouts. It was a loud, unfriendly commotion.

Spinning around, Lang left his pack in the bushes and cocked his body forward slightly, pulling his head down between his shoulders, and edged back toward the group. He stayed low along the edge of the thicket to remain out of sight for as long as possible. From a distance, he could see that three men—

obviously hostile—were confronting his friends, and one of them had what looked to Lang like an AK-47 pointed at Peter. The other men held long knives in front of them, pointing them at the women in a threatening manner.

The three hostiles were dressed like accountants. That detail was shocking to see. Almost unbelievable. Except for a lack of ties (one of which was tied around an arm of one of the men holding a knife, as if it were a tourniquet), the men looked as though they might have been out to lunch at an Applebee's and together had decided to hike into the forest and rob someone at gunpoint. They weren't dressed for the elements at all, but they had weapons. The incongruity was alarming. They were using the weapons to threaten, waving them like spreadsheets in a boardroom melee.

Lang approached from behind the men, and Peter saw him, and Lang saw that he saw, but the older man gave him no sign that he could interpret as an instruction, so the young man crept just a little bit closer. Almost imperceptibly, Peter indicated with a slight motion of the hand that he wanted Lang to *stop* as the man with the AK-47 began shouting that he wanted Peter and Natasha to throw over their backpacks.

Lang froze, unsure whether Peter wanted him to just stand quietly, or move to cover. In such moments, you have to decide one way or another. So Lang decided on the latter, and, as he moved slowly toward a nearby tree, his foot snapped a fallen branch that lay buried under the snow. The crack of the wood alerted the three bandits to his presence, and instantly bodies moved into motion and events seemed to slow down for everyone involved.

The man with the AK-47 wheeled around to see who was behind him, and Peter, reacting with shocking speed and agility, crashed into the man and they tumbled over into the snow. Peter snapped the weapon from his hands with little trouble at all as Lang rushed to help. In that moment, the two knife-wielding bandits took advantage of the scuffle to snap up the two backpacks, and, before anyone could shout or protest, they had bounded awkwardly into the forest. They left without looking back for their colleague, sprinting into the woods, slipping and sliding on their flat leather dress shoes, winding in and out of the trees... and they made their escape.

Lang never even thought about giving chase. The man who had held the AK-47 jumped up to his feet. He looked at Peter with a murderous gleam in his eye and demanded that Peter give him his gun back. *Demanded it.* If it had happened more slowly, Peter would have stopped to laugh at him. Here was a thief that had, seconds before, been threatening to kill him over a couple of backpacks, and now he was brazenly demanding that the weapon used in his crime be returned to him, as if some cosmic injustice had occurred. In that instant, the man realized that life, indeed, could turn on a dime.

Peter didn't have time to react with shock and amazement. The man rushed at him, apparently in the expectation that Peter wouldn't know how to work the gun. In this, he was wrong. Peter gracefully stepped backward a half step as the man flailed toward him, causing the charging man to miss him. Peter pivoted, just a small twist on his rear leg, and swung his body around so that the direction the barrel pointed was not towards Lang, or Natasha, or Elsie... but instead the gun was pointed off in the direction the two other men had run. When the attacker recovered from his missed lunge, he spun back around and rushed at Peter, again. And... as simply and effortlessly as one might drop a dime, Peter shot him point-blank in the chest.

The bullet hit the man in the center of his mass. The sound of the blast ricocheted off the snow, climbed up into the mountain, and spun around in the cool, crisp air. The man fell backward, into the snow, and he died.

\* \* \* \*

Peter didn't spend any time at all frozen in place, or grieving over what he'd done. He simply checked to make sure that Elsie, Natasha, and Lang were alright. He looked up for a moment, as if he might chase the other two bandits into the woods to retrieve the backpacks, but he decided against it. At his age and in his condition, he probably would not catch them, and he'd definitely leave his three friends in danger. If the bandits were working with anyone else, it would not be wise to split his group. In any event, the time lost would not benefit anyone. The two packs were simply gone. He shook his head as if to apologize.

Peter quickly made a mental rundown of the situation. They'd gained a battle rifle, but at immense cost. He was not sure that he would have made that trade. He worried about the loss of medicines and food, but what was done was done. And they still had Lang's pack.

*Lang's pack!*

"Lang! Where is your backpack, son?"

"Oh! Uh... I left it in the trees when I heard the ruckus. I'll run back and get it."

"No. Wait, Lang," Peter said, firmly. "We'll go together."

Walking over to retrieve the pack, Peter checked the weapon, pulled out the clip and felt the heft so he could determine its capacity and estimate how many rounds were likely in it. His mind continued cataloging, prioritizing, and planning. Killing the bandit in self-defense was something he'd had to do, and this was not the time to fret over things that could not be undone.

With the pack retrieved, they walked back to the body of the dead accountant, and Peter knelt and began frisking the corpse. In his pockets, he found a cell phone (dead), car keys (useless), a pen (useful), and a tube of chapstick (useful). Actually, he thought, the phone and the keys were useful for other things, too, so stuck them into the side pockets of his pants. As he did so, he made a mental note that the man had all of these things with him that were, for someone like him, now *useless*... but he did not have a lighter or a knife. *What kind of man doesn't carry the simple things that he should have with him at all times?* Peter shook his head. *But what kind of man lets such a man sneak up on him in broad daylight?*

The dead man had no wallet, or, at least he had no wallet on him. As he finished the quick frisk, Peter looked up at Lang when he noticed the wedding ring on the man's finger. *Gold.* He slipped it off with some difficulty, and, catching Elsie's wince, he looked at her without shame on his face. "This will pay for what his friends stole." He adopted a tone that was not angry or scolding, but was instructional and encouraging. He hoped that she was the kind of person who could take patient instruction.

"Sentimental notions like leaving gold on the ground while thieves run through the forest with our property... those have no place among us anymore. We certainly need to keep our humanity, but humanity has been accompanied with a large dosage of sentimental stupidity of late." He waved his hand as if in accusation at the world. "All *this*... this collapse... it is all a part of the result of that kind of madness. We didn't steal from this man. We didn't provoke him, or cause him to do evil things. He *made* me kill him. He would have kept coming at me until I did... which amplifies his guilt."

Peter studied her face to see how she was taking his words.

"We need to be able to replace our gear at some point, and we'll need to buy it from someone, since *we* will not use *our* guns to steal. This is merely recompense for the trouble he has caused us."

He looked around again at the faces of the others, scanning for understanding. All three of his friends nodded at him. He might have seen, though he probably did not, that they were even grateful. As they searched their hearts, they found a willingness to let the strongest among them carry not only the heaviest burden but also the weightiest questions. Peter showed, by his demeanor, that he, too, was grateful. With a sideways smile he indicated that he realized that part of the reason they now found themselves in this predicament, having their food and medicine sprinting away from them in the hands of interlopers, was that he had allowed himself a moment of all-too human frailty and had relaxed his watch. He tried to reassure them with his eyes that he felt his burden and accepted it, and that he would not let it happen again.

With that, the four turned on their heels, turned back up the mountain, and headed toward the southwest, continuing their climb.

\* \* \* \*

An hour after the incident, they stopped for rest and decided to eat some food. They only had Lang's backpack now, and Natasha carried it so that Peter could wield the rifle more easily. Lang's arm was beginning to hurt him, and Elsie was wheezing from the long, slow climb up the mountain.

Peter hiked out a few hundred feet into the woods and picked a good place to hide himself so that he could stand guard while the others rested and ate. The other three did not sit clumped together in a group despite the fact that Peter stood guard over them. They kept themselves spread out by several yards, just far enough apart so that they could still talk and interact while minimizing the likelihood that a sniper or attacker, should there be one out there somewhere, could get to them all at once. They opened up the bag and pulled out some foil packs of tuna, and Natasha went through the process of starting a small fire to warm them and to boil and purify more water.

After a half hour, Lang went and took the rifle and replaced Peter so that Peter could eat and rest awhile. Before the two men parted, Lang stopped Peter and indicated that they should both squat down so that they could maintain some cover while they spoke. Lang winced a little when he knelt down, and Peter noticed it.

"How are you doing, Lang."

"I'm alright. Just a little sore and tired. But I'll make it."

"We're going to have to stop at some point and take a look at that wound."

"I know, but listen... that's not why I want to speak to you."

"Oh? Is something wrong?" Peter asked.

"Peter..." Lang started. He paused and thought for a second as he looked around, his head on a swivel, remaining vigilant even while they spoke. Peter did the same, but at this point, their eyes met. "Peter... I know you blame yourself for what happened back there... us falling into the hands of those bandits. I know you do..."

Peter tried to interrupt him, but Lang stopped him with a raise of his hand.

"Listen to me, Peter, and I'll say what I want to say. We need to keep this short. I don't expect a reply or an argument."

Lang was only eighteen, but he had matured more in the last few days than in all of the previous years of his life combined. Peter recognized this, nodded, and looked downwards for a second.

"I know you blame yourself for that, and, well... we *do* need to be more vigilant if we want to survive. I get all of that. Nevertheless, no man can keep us perfectly safe in this new world. No man. There are four of us, and in these woods, and... now this country... there are simply too many people to expect we won't run across someone. Starving people, angry people, criminal people, lonely people..." he paused again, giving his statement some weight. "The best team of Special Forces soldiers in the world couldn't guarantee that they won't stumble into a firefight or an ambush. No amount of being alert is going to guarantee that. Nor can anyone guarantee that we won't die out here. In fact, just the opposite is true. We will *all* die some time... We can't cover this team the way it should be covered, and we don't know the terrain. The hostile forces out there outnumber us by the millions. Let's not fall prey to this notion that just because we have guns and a little training there will be no mistakes, or that we can't be surprised and overwhelmed."

Peter looked up at him, nodding, but did not speak, so Lang continued.

"I just want you to know that none of us expects you to be God. We need to learn from our mistakes and get better, but only a fool would think that anyone could do much better than you've done. After all, and... I mean this with the utmost in love and respect, Peter... but, after all, you are a middle-aged man who has been out of practice for a decade or more. In addition, you're shepherding three people who have little more than desk training and theory. Natasha and I? Our training was in spycraft and deception, not in wilderness survival or unit defense tactics. So don't be too hard on yourself... okay?"

Peter looked at him and closed his eyes for a moment. He was very thankful to hear Lang's words, like a man given permission to be human, with all his frailties intact. He reached out, grabbed Lang's hand, and allowed the young man to lift him as he stood and shook out his creaky bones. "Okay, my son." He smiled into the eyes of his young friend. He lightly patted Lang on his good shoulder, then walked back toward the camp and left Lang to watch and guard.

\* \* \* \*

While he lay down to sleep for a short nap, Natasha and Elsie talked more about their situation, what they hoped to find if they succeeded in reaching Amish country, telling the small tales of life that had led them to this point, branching off into the wilderness of conversation as old friends might. Each of them encouraged the other to stay strong, to be more vigilant, and to persevere.

"Peter saved us yet again," Natasha whispered, smiling at the man huddled in the snow with his head propped up by a smooth rock.

"I get the feeling that he is very fond of you and Lang, and that he is glad to be able to protect you and to take care for you," Elsie replied.

"He is a good man," Natasha said. She looked on him fondly, and wondered how she had never noticed his gentle side before.

"I see that."

"He's lost his family, and we're all he really has."

"Oh!" Elsie started, "were they—?"

"No. No. I'm sorry," Natasha said. "They left long ago. He hasn't seen them in twenty years."

"Divorce, then?"

"No. Oh... Listen... Elsie, I'm sorry," Natasha said, suddenly remembering that, even though they had already passed through a great deal together in a short time, it was not her place to share Peter's story if he didn't want it known. "I probably shouldn't be talking about him. I shouldn't have said anything. It's his business to tell you about himself as he sees fit. I just..." she stammered, embarrassed for having taken the conversation into more private concerns, "I just wanted you to know that he is a very good man."

"I do know. I see that," Elsie said, smiling. "So, my dear, let's just leave it at that." She looked at Natasha and gave her the kind of loving smile that a mother gives a daughter. Natasha noticed it, and she was happy to have seen it.

Just as the two women finished their conversation, they heard the sharp crack of a small-caliber rifle being fired. Peter jumped to his feet, just in time to see Lang sauntering into camp swinging a white rabbit that he'd shot with the .22 Marlin. Without saying a word, Lang tossed the rabbit so that it landed within a few feet of the fire, and, keeping his head on a swivel and his eyes alive, he turned softly and walked back to his station to stand guard.

# Chapter 8
# Carbondale

Peter figured that they were within thirty minutes of reaching the outskirts of Carbondale when, while coming over a low-rising hill, they happened upon three men sitting around a fire. Peter saw them first, and the three men saw Peter's gun almost immediately.

Two of the men leapt up from the log they were sitting on and sprinted away as though they were acting out of pure instinct. The third, reacting more slowly, sat frozen in place for a moment. He watched the four hikers approach him, and he finally rose to his feet and began backing away while keeping his eyes on them. Peter lowered the weapon, raised up a hand and tried to indicate with his eyes and his actions that he meant no harm.

The man looked uncertain, as if he were about to run after his mates, when Lang said calmly, "Listen, sir, we mean you no harm. You can go peacefully, or call your friends and have them return to your fire. We're just traveling through. We didn't see you from further away, due to the hill, or we would have avoided you. We have no desire to hurt anyone. And we're not bandits. We're simply passing on."

"Umm..." the man sputtered, his eyes racing from point to point as his mind flipped through his options and the probabilities attached to each. "Yes. Well, okay then. I'll just... I'll just go get them. They won't have gone far. I'll be right back."

The man began to walk nervously away through the trees, almost as if he expected Peter to shoot him in the back at any moment. After a few seconds of this trepidations walking, he broke out into a run as though the anxiety was simply too much.

"Do you think he'll come back? Elsie asked.

"I don't know," Peter replied. He looked at Elsie, then at Natasha and Lang and shrugged his shoulders, as if to say, "This is what life is like now."

"What can you do?" Peter said. "Everyone is spooked. And they should be. These people seem harmless enough, but keep your eyes on them and watch their every movement. Watch how they interact with one another. Be looking for clues that perhaps they are not as harmless as they look."

Before long, the three men came walking back sheepishly through the woods. They did not look malevolent, but they were very nervous, like cattle, hungry but cautious.

Lang spoke first. "We apologize for interrupting you. As I am sure that your friend here has told you, we're just traveling through. We mean no harm at all. We've seen our share of death and violence, and we understand your concerns. We've lost our homes, and we're traveling into Pennsylvania to meet up with some friends."

One of the men, the one who had been too slow to escape at first, shuffled his feet in the snow and then looked up at Peter, and then at Lang. He nodded his head to the two women with them, as if by way of formal greeting.

"Well, if you are traveling into Pennsylvania, you'll be glad to know that you've been there for some time. We came from Carbondale, just over that hill. You can see it from up-top there." He pointed along a ridgeline to the southwest and squinted into the sun.

Lang nodded at the man, thanking him. "We don't intend to go there—not into town—but if you have any news you'd be willing to share, we'd appreciate it. At some point we're going to have to find some supplies or—at the very least—some way to find out what's in front of us..." He left a kind of open-ended invitation hanging in the air for the men to tell them anything they found to be appropriate.

"I'll tell you," the man said, with a bitterness that verged on anger barely disguised in his voice. His visceral passion was surprising to the four hikers. "You don't want to go anywhere *near* Carbondale. In fact, we're still too close to it for my own comfort..." He looked sideways at his colleagues, and Peter judged that their proximity to the city had been a matter of some debate as they'd sat around their campfire. "And as for supplies, I think you're gonna be out of luck, man."

"What's going on in Carbondale?"

The three men exchanged looks that betrayed a shared experience, and in their looks, Peter saw what he could only call *fear*. The air between them dripped with anxiety and concern.

"The town's been taken over by the National Guard." One of the men snorted at the mention of that name. "*Supposedly*," the man said, making quotes around the word with his fingers, "they did it to help feed and shelter refugees pouring into the area from New York and the surrounding area. A couple of weeks ago, the town had about 9,000 people living in it. It was nice. We grew up there," the man said, making a little waving motion with his fingers, pointing back and forth between his mates. "Industrial, but nice. Anyway, it was a little outlying suburb of Scranton. But..." the man's voice halted a bit, and he closed his eyes for a few seconds before he started talking again. "Scranton is gone. It's just *gone*. Burned to the ground. And now there are over 100,000 people in what can only be called an internment camp. Something like out of the war." He didn't say which war, but, judging by their age, Peter guessed that he probably meant the one their grandfathers had likely fought in, the Second World War. "There are thousands more arriving by day and by night. It's a hellhole."

"What do you mean? How so?" Lang asked. He reached up and soothed his aching shoulder as he did, feeling the heat of the wound radiate along his arm.

Another man picked up the conversation and answered. There was anger in his voice as well. "The place has turned into nothing more than a prison camp. The National Guard unit running the place was up from Missouri to help in the emergency following Hurricane Sandy and the Nor'easter. They were working in New York, I believe. When all the power went out and the authority structure broke down... whatever that was that knocked out all the lights... they just took control. Rolled through here and began knocking people around. They supply the camp by doing raids in the surrounding area. They rob *farms*, loot whatever *stores* are left ... kill people in their *homes*." The man relayed this information as though he himself couldn't quite believe it, emphasizing at the end of each phrase a kind of incredulity, as though there had been something sacred in the very mention of such places.

"It's hard to know how it all got started. People were standing around outside the main grocery in my neighborhood bumming cigarettes and sharing news, when these trucks just rolled into town. From a distance, we thought it was the power company. Hell, everybody cheered! But... no one is cheering anymore."

One of his mates kicked a rock and looked off in the distance, over the ridge, toward the city. "Ain't that the truth," he muttered, under his breath, to no one in particular.

"There was a group of homesteaders... whaddya call'em? *Survivalists?* They lived in this little community back in the woods a bit. The Guard just wiped that place out. We saw that with our own eyes as we were hiking out this way. They came in and commandeered all the supplies, fuel, goods... even the people. In the first few days, they interrogated people, treating them like *prisoners...* They asked and prodded and even tortured people until they found out where these end of the world types were, you know, the people who had stored up food and supplies... Then the guardsman sent out the word that people who did that were '*hoarders.*' That's what they called them. Then they outlawed hoarding and announced the death penalty as a punishment. I'm telling you," the man shook his head, "I wouldn't have believed it if I hadn't seen it."

Peter took in what they said and didn't ask questions. He was calculating how to adjust the trajectory of their hike in relation to this news. One of the men, the first one who had spoken, now chimed in again, pointing to Peter's weapon and the one Lang had slung over his good shoulder. "Those guns. You better be careful with those. The Guard has been shooting on site anyone caught with guns and ammo. They don't even ask questions. They simply fire and then relieve you of your burden. And they have snipers posted at outposts all around the town." He nodded at Peter as he said this, as if to promise him that what he was saying was true. "They shoot first and ask questions later, buddy. And they rob and steal at will, and they are deadly efficient at it."

"Lord, have mercy on us!" Elsie said, almost involuntarily. Her gloved hand covered her mouth and her eyes betrayed her fear.

"Well, you better hope that the Lord does, because the people running Carbondale will not."

Lang scratched his chin. He, too, was considering this new information. He had learned from Volkhov to dig deeper, and so he did. "And they *all* went along with it? The whole National Guard unit?"

"Oh, no," the second man replied. "That's just it. There was... there *is*... a battle going on over that very thing. That's one of the problems right now. It's hard to tell who is who. There was a large portion of the Missouri Guard unit that wouldn't go along with the plan, and they've kind of formed themselves into, I don't know... what would you call it?" He looked at his friends and they shrugged. "...A resistance unit?" His friends shrugged again. "They call themselves the FMA, the Free Missouri Army. Man," he said, shaking his head, "you can't make this stuff up. Only a few weeks ago I was buying milk on the way home for my wife, and now we have armies battling in our streets. A lot of former cops and ex-military... those are the ones that don't seem to be going along with the Guard's tyranny." He looked at one of his friends. "Well, dang it, it *is* tyranny," he said, obviously continuing some argument the two had been having. "You can call it *temporary measures* if you want, but it ain't temporary for those folks lying in the ground."

Turning his back to his friend, he continued. "Anyway... so, there is a group that has set themselves up as an alternative, and they do seem to be more reasonable. If nothing else, they have local folks involved. And this FMA is the only hope that a lot of rural people have around here of not being forced into the camps. So right now, we're all in the middle of a little 'civil war', and it really just comes down to who you run into."

Peter sighed deeply and looked at Lang. The two men raised their eyebrows at each other, and each waited for the other to speak.

Peter spoke first, and he spoke to his group.

"I suppose we should head straight west. We'll have to find some way to cross Interstate 81, and that might be worse than Highway 17 was, but if we make it we can turn south. It'll be a longer walk that way, but we'll avoid a lot more trouble, and it seems to me like the farther we get away from Carbondale, the better."

Lang nodded his head, and then turned back to the three men.

"You said we can see Carbondale from the top of that hill? Is it safe to take a look?"

"Probably," one of the men said. "As I said, there are snipers here and there... or at least we have heard that there are. Hell, most of what we have just told you is hearsay, except for what we've seen with our own eyes... but what we did see was bad enough. So you prolly want to lie down and keep low and don't stay on the ridge very long."

"I'd like to check it out, if that's alright with you, Peter?"

"Yes. I think I'd like to see it too, but, you go ahead. I'll stay here with the ladies." He looked at the three men and smiled, before adding, "No offense of course."

"None taken."

\* \* \* \*

Lang walked up the hill, and as he walked, he noticed that the pain in his shoulder had increased. Perhaps it was the standing around. The constant walking gave him focus and took his mind off the pain, but the time spent standing and talking caused him to feel every movement of the wound. He could feel the ache throb through him like a knife. It pulsed with his heartbeat, and the pain spiked if he breathed too deeply.

As he reached the top of the hill, he dropped down on all fours in the snow and crawled the last bit until he crested the plateau. Looking down on the city, he inhaled sharply at the sight and felt the pain shoot through him, even down into his lower back.

Spread out before him was a landscape only seen, in our age, in the movies. There was an encampment consisting of thousands of large tents pooled in the middle of a low-slung valley. Sitting up on the hill was the highway that wound around a mountain and ran through the heart of what used to be Carbondale. The camp was bordered on all sides by trenches dug into the earth... scratched in, really... with razor-sharp wire strung along the borders and watchtowers being constructed at the four-corners by people being herded through their labors by men with guns. Along the outside of the fence, men and women were digging the trench deeper, and the occasional guardsman placed around the perimeter shouted orders to hasten the work.

The town was a direct likeness of a World War II era Nazi prison camp. There were tents stretching almost as far as the eye could see, and prisoners, most of them in clothes better meant for the city, were trudging through the gates and wandering aimlessly along the inner areas of the fence, as if they were plotting an escape, or hoping that the fences would hold fast against whatever terrors had attended their way to the camp.

Off to the east... placed, it seemed, so that the newly arriving refugees had to trudge through it on their way to the camp, was a fresh cemetery, a burial ground for the thousands of dead. Diggers worked feverishly in the snow.

Lang pierced his lips, blinked his eyes, and surveyed the scene. He thought about the two graves he'd already had to dig in the snow, and he knew that the ground was getting harder day by day. That wasn't the only reason he felt sympathy for the people down below, of course, but it was one reason. He knew how hard their work was and how much harder it would become.

Pretty soon, he thought to himself, those people are going to have to find something else to do with the bodies.

# Chapter 9
# Trek

"Hey, wait! Let me turn it up. That's my jam!"

Calvin Rhodes ran across the painted concrete floor and slid the last four feet, the brand new leather soles of his Tony Lama boots sliding, almost frictionless, to a stop at the edge of the floor-length toolbox. He reached up, cranked the handle on the radio/CD player, and then swiveled on the pointed toes of his boots, grabbing a ratchet from an open drawer in the process and using it as a microphone while he broke into a rap that betrayed a hint of accent from his Chinese heritage.

*"Yo, microphone check... one, two. What is this? The five foot assassin with the ruffneck bizness."*

His companion, the older man leaning over the engine of an old Ford pick-up, looked up and wiped the grease from his hands on his jeans. He laughed as Calvin did a little dance across the floor, throwing his knee out to the side and then pulling his hips into alignment, waving his free hand above his head and giving a little hop. He looked like a bony windmill-like contraption, or one of those air puppets that you might have seen, not long ago, in front of party stores.

"Cal, you're a clown. That song is older than you are! You got moves, though... I'll give you that." The old man changed his smile into a look of mock seriousness. "Okay, young man, we have to get busy. I'm fixin' to see if I can get this thing started."

Calvin stopped his dance and came over to the front of the truck, leaning in studiously to let the man tell him what he was doing.

"Now, this thing runs pretty simply. It's four on the floor, and as long as you keep some coolant in the radiator and check your oil as you go, it should get you where you're going. It's not gonna win you any speed contests, and the only lights I have workin' are the headlights, but if you'll look here..." the man pointed down to the front of the motor and then traced with his finger towards the back of the engine compartment, "...I've been able to replace all the belts and spark plugs... put in new filters." He paused. "And the tires are good. She should be fine."

Calvin looked into the engine. He was like most American young men his age and had almost no idea what he was looking at or what the mechanic was talking about. He'd been brought up in a time when cars ran on computers, as if by magic, and he wanted to ask questions so he could know what to do if the engine stopped, but he didn't even know where to begin. The man saw the doubt in his eyes.

Calvin looked at the man a little sheepishly. "I know that once upon a time men were both drivers and mechanics. But *my* generation..." Calvin was searching for the words when the old man helped him. "Well, you've done the first poorly, and the second not at all." Calvin shook his head. "Yeah...

They just became so complicated. I mean, if you can't do it on a video game..." he paused and the old man thought, *well that won't be a problem anymore...*

"I've just never even tried to work on them."

"Relax, Cal. Compared to those new machines, this ol' dog is a bicycle." He fiddled with a connection on the distributor cap until he was satisfied and then closed the hood.

"This here is the Ranger model of the 1965 Ford F-100. It was a new thing in its day, and they only made a handful of 'em. This special model had bucket seats, which was pretty unique for a pickup truck back in them days." The old man walked around the front of the pickup toward the toolbox, cleaning a socket wrench with a rag as he walked. "It had carpeting, which has since been worn out, and a curtain that covered the gas tank behind the seats." He sorted through the open drawer, found the tool he was looking for, and then turned to Calvin. "It has a couple hunnerd thousand miles on her, but it didn't get there by not being solid. Long as you keep gas in the tank and don't get in a hurry, and don't git y'self killed along the way, it'll get you to Pennsylvania."

Calvin shrugged and smiled at the older man. "I have no doubt. I just hope I can find gas between here and there."

"Well, that's just the thing. You're man and me... we're gonna set you up with a couple of stops along the way that'll take care of your needs in that regard. This thing has been outfitted with a twenty-gallon tank, and I'm going to put as many gas cans as I can muster in the bed, covered by a tarp. That'll get you as far as, maybe, Memphis." He pointed to the running boards along the pickup's short bed. "Now, those things there might get you into trouble. If you run into anyone on the road, don't let 'em get close enough to jump in the back using those things. I've turned the rotors and replaced all the pads so the brakes shouldn't give you any trouble, but you'll have to be awful certain that you don't get into any wrecks or stop too soon. If you do..." he brought his hands up into fists and splayed his fingers and then his hands out in a slow-motion pantomime... "Poof."

"I got ya."

"Now look here, Calvin... you're not gonna wanna to stop for nothin', right? There are bad folks out there and they ain't as nice as you are. You gotta get this package to your man's folks up in P.A." The way he said that made Calvin smile... *peeyay*. "There are people that'll try to stop you just for something to divert themselves. Once you hit that road, you put your ears back and go. You hear what I'm tellin' you?" Calvin nodded. He understood that it was an important mission that he'd been entrusted with, and he was glad to do it.

"Believe me, this truck is gonna be the fanciest thing on the road. Everything else out there... all those automobiles that were dependent on a centralized electric nervous system... they've recently met with their death—powered *down* for the last time. However, the ol' dog here, she's in her prime. Even with the springs pokin' up through the seat cushions, you're gonna be ridin' on a gold mine. That's the reason I've kept her around for all these years." He ran his hand along the rusted fender as lovingly as a mother might stroke the hair of her child. "That, and the fact that my granddaddy drove it, and he didn't leave my dad much besides it. Then my dad left it to me..." He paused, his mind gone elsewhere, and then came back to himself. "So anyhow, son, now... I'm leaving it to you. You take care of her and she'll take care of you." The older man placed his hand on the young orphan's shoulder, this boy whom he'd come to know and love as if he was his own son.

Calvin gulped. He didn't much like displays of emotion, even if it was coming from the man who'd largely raised him. He was about to blush, and he could feel it, when he became aware of the sound of a screen door slamming over near the main house and the crunch of footsteps walking on the gravel across the yard toward the garage. He heard the radio wind down to the chorus, as a Tribe Called Quest rapped about how they were buggin' out. He saw the pretty, young face of the girl he'd come to think of as his sister as it rounded the corner into the open doorway. She stood silhouetted in the frame of light, cleared her throat, and told him that Jonathan Wall was standing in the kitchen and wanted to talk to him.

\* \* \* \*

Stephen sat in the dark and listened to his mother breathing. Ever since they'd heard someone try to break into their bunker early that morning, his mother had been a bundle of nerves, but he'd finally convinced her to lie down and take a nap while he continued to prepare things for their escape.

They would take a couple of bikes, some sets of the hazmat gear, and as much food and water as they could haul with them. They'd carry whatever they could load onto their backs and onto the bikes and still be able to ride safely and swiftly. The plan was to take their gear and flee southward, out of the city. They both admitted that it was a crazy gambit, but what else could they do?

While inspecting the place, Stephen's mother had discovered that the bunker had an open airway at the back of the storeroom, a small pipe that lead somewhere that they couldn't figure. That fact made their plan to shelter there as bad as being outside... because, who knew if that airway was filtered, or—even if it was—if the filtration system even worked?

"We need to get as far away from here as we can get," she'd said. "This place won't do us any good against what I fear is coming. And worse, if someone with a little more sense or a better tool than a shoulder tries to break down the door, we're sitting ducks."

"I understand," Stephen had said, "but why isn't this place built better? Why would somebody go to the trouble of building a bunker that doesn't protect you from the very thing it's supposed to?"

"Peace of mind, Stephen. Or marketing. Back during the cold war, there were people getting rich building facilities that they sold to people based on their fears. They'd weave a swell story, tell the people how only *they* could fix a problem, and then they'd come in and throw up some half-designed thing that would seem to the uninformed to suit their needs. Most people just want to *think* they are safe. That's always true, Stephen. It doesn't really matter whether they are actually safe or not. The same applies to a lot of the survival industry. Companies sell cheaply made goods that wouldn't do what they were advertised to do even if the sellers *had* intended them to. A lot of them simply push products to make a buck. Castles in the air." Veronica paused. She knew her rants sometimes disturbed the boy, so she got back to the point. "Of course, we don't know if that happened here or not. Maybe that airway has a fallout filter on it and is perfectly fine. That's just the point, boy, we don't know. The airflow seems to be a bit too free for me to feel safe about it. Maybe it was just a design flaw, or a contingency plan, or something that, in all those years of lying dormant, got uncovered... either way, this place is useless to us now because we can't trus' it. We'll have to leave."

Now they were just waiting for nightfall before venturing out, and his mother had finally drifted into a fitful sleep. Stephen had unpacked and repacked their bags, putting in the things his mother had laid out for him. He hummed to himself quietly while doing so, drumming his fingers on the tops of the boxes in the storeroom. He thought of his iPod and his

CDs and his video games and wished he had a guitar and had learned to play it.

He listened to his mother breathing, and wondered how long it would be before he could live, once again, in a world of music.

\* \* \* \*

The campfire crackled when the log split open and tiny embers flew up into the air, rising on a small puff of wind and lifting toward heaven before burning themselves out and disappearing into small bits of ash.

Four men sat looking into the fire and calculating how much food they had left and how far it would take them. Three of the men had set out on their journey together, and they had a bond that seemed solidified by some past history, perhaps the commission of a crime, while the fourth had joined them by happenstance. It was clear from the tenor of the conversation that, despite their journey thus far, the fourth remained the odd man out.

"Mike, we need to pick up our pace if we are going to get out of these mountains before our food runs out," Val said. Val was a hulking brute of a man, and gave off an air of one who ought not to be trifled with.

"Relax, Val. I know what I'm doing... and listen, try to use contractions more. For example, instead of 'if *we are* going to get out of these mountains,' you'd say, "if *we're* going to get out of these mountains.' Americans use more contractions and speak more lazily and fluidly. You sound like a robot." Mike looked at Val and didn't quite smile. His eyes smiled, but did so with a hint of authority and superiority. He continued...

"We don't have much farther to go before we'll be in an area where we can find shelter, and we have enough food to last a couple more days." Mike was short and stocky. He was clearly the brains of the group of three men who'd initially headed out into the wilderness together. The third man, Steve, seemed to be mere window dressing. But not like in a clothing store. More like a mannequin you'd find on display in a hardware store or in outdoor gear store. The strong silent type, with a heavy emphasis on *silent.*

"Steve, would you like a little more stew? I think we have enough for everyone to have another bite."

Steve nodded and held out his cup.

"Ken?" Val asked, offering him the spoon.

"Oh, for heaven's sake! It's Kent!" Kent was the fourth man. The outsider. He made a point of spitting the last letter off his teeth. "Kent. The 'T' is *not* silent. If we're going to call each other by new names, the least you could do is try and get the name right," the round-faced man said, his eyes burning with fire. It was clear that he didn't like Val, and from the way the brute arched his back at the tone of Kent's voice, one could tell that the feeling was mutual. Val turned to face Kent, squaring his shoulders as the smaller man sat forward on the log and seemed about to rise.

Mike smoothed their ruffled feathers. "Gentlemen! Give it a rest. We have a while still to travel, yet. Perhaps you can learn to get along better so that Steve and I," he made a nod to the silent man to his left, "don't have to douse the both of you."

"I can't help it, Mike. He burns me." Val made a motion toward the smaller man as if he would slap him with the back of his hand if he didn't have better self-control, and it wasn't clear that he really did. The round-faced man didn't flinch, and his eyes betrayed no fear. He simply sat and looked back at Val and spread his hands. He made them into fists and did a little punching motion into the air, and then, turning away, he looked with boredom into the fire. Reflexively, he reached up and removed his glasses and began to clean them.

\*\*\*\*

Calvin Rhodes was born in Austin, Texas, in 1994, where his parents had been attending the University of Texas on student visas. His father, a Chinese pharmaceutical engineer, had come to the states to complete a graduate degree program, sponsored by the Chinese government in an ongoing effort to reform China's national healthcare system. His mother, a musician, had died during childbirth, and thus his father had to raise him alone.

When it came to being a single father and trying to maintain his course work, Cal's father had been completely lost from the very start. In fact, he would have simply withdrawn from the university and returned home to China to enlist his family's help with the child, except for the mildly aggressive way his embassy office had handled the news of his wife's passing. Gently, but firmly, and with no room left for doubt, the consular attaché told him that he was to continue his studies. A small stipend was provided so that he could secure childcare, but nothing else was offered by way of help... certainly not understanding.

Cal's father had done the best he could. One of the things he'd done while he was looking for answers and for strength to face his struggles, was turn to the search for spirituality. He'd never been a particularly religious man, making his way in the Chinese system by offering the kind of public acceptance of science as the supreme answer for everything. While he secretly admitted to an appreciation for traditional Chinese medical practices, and he had a deep and abiding faith in certain ancient Chinese cultural mores, he'd been successful in his career, to the point that some in the Chinese politburo were eying him for regional directorships, precisely because he'd been a man of industry and science and not mythology. He'd been exactly the type of man the country needed as China moved toward more Western-style medical standards. At a minimum, he was good at managing business, a useful thing in a time when the pharmaceutical business in his country was on the ascent.

Still, there was the matter of the boy. Calvin was a fussy baby. From his very earliest days, he behaved as though he took it as a personal affront that his mother wasn't there for him. This was understandable, but it didn't make matters any better for the harried young man trying to raise him. The fact that Cal's father had proved to be only a middling student made things even worse. In order to advance, he'd been forced to spend many hours reading and rereading texts that other students simply seemed to grasp at first glance.

Perhaps the turning point for Calvin's father was the day he'd received, in the mail, from his family back home, a small book by a moral philosopher named Li Hongzhi. This philosopher had recently become famous in China for developing a movement founded on traditional Chinese physical exercises combined with the practice of certain moral beliefs. Chief among these beliefs were truthfulness, compassion, and forbearance. The book had changed Calvin's father forever.

The pharmaceutical engineer became a member of the outlaw movement that eventually became known as Falun Gong.

Drawing strength from his new-found religion—if it could rightly be called a religion—Calvin's father threw himself into his tasks. He took to his studies with a new found vigor and seemed to grow in his role as a father in a way that surprised even his family back in China, as well as the few friends he'd made on campus. He became, in short, a zealot, and that zealotry infused him with energy.

All of this is by way of explaining why, on a day he'd taken to get out of the city and tour the beautiful hill country he'd heard so much about, he was doing his exercises in a small park next to the *Vereins Kirch* in Fredericksburg, Texas, and not caring a whit for the stares that he got from the people in that small tourist town.

People were not used to seeing a Chinese man with a toddler at his side standing in the middle of an artsy Texas village next to an old Colonial-era Lutheran Church moving his body as if he were pushing the wind. The folks walking by stole their furtive glances and tried not to stop and stare. They were polite in their peering insouciance, but if one had stood to the side and watched, it would have been clear that their reaction was unimportant to Calvin's father. He was impervious to even their walking amazement.

One young man in his later teens, standing in the park, did not steal furtive glances or peer through the side of his eyes at the Chinese man's antics. That man noticed both the crowd and the man's practiced disregard of them. He knew what it was like to be watched sideways and marginalized, and he figured that if you were going to look at a man, you should just go on and look at him.

His name was Jonathan Wall.

# Chapter 10
# Bridges

"Stephen, we have a serious problem."

Veronica looked at her son with her fists on her hips, frowning—not at him particularly—but at the problem.

"We have to ride south through Brooklyn, and that will be difficult enough, boy, but then we have to cross the Verrazano Bridge, and that could be next to impossible. The bridge will almost certainly be blocked by bandits; people who will want to take our bikes; people who will steal our food if we will let them; people who might want to take our lives."

"You think it will be that bad, mom?" Stephen asked. He concentrated on making sure that his face showed bravery and masked his fear.

Veronica noticed Stephen's efforts and she was pleased. *Half of any hard victory consists of overcoming the fears that might keep us from the battle in the first place,* she thought.

"I think it will be worse than I think it will be," she said, smiling.

"What's the plan?"

"Getting over the bridge is the first thing. We'll take our battles one at a time. We need to be prepared to ride fast and yet carefully. Watch for trash on the roadways, son, nails in particular. A flat tire on your bike makes it as useless as not having one. I found spare tubes in the storeroom, but there will be no time or place to stop and change them. We need to avoid anything that will keep us from getting out of here quickly."

Stephen looked at his mother, wanting to mention a thought that had occurred to him. While she was sleeping, he'd been silently drumming because drumming always seemed to help him think clearly. As his hands worked the rhythm in his head, his mind flashed back to a day when he'd been riding the subway. Beating the heels of his hands like a madman on the tops of his knees, keeping time to a song playing in his ears, he'd looked up and noticed that people had slid away from him on the seats, leaving him alone at the end of the train.

"What if we put on the fallout gear now?" he said, smiling. "It will freak people out. They'll think we're scientists or something, or maybe from the government... or that we're sick. Maybe they'll leave us alone."

"Boy," Veronica said, placing her long thin fingers on his cheek and giving his nose a little tweak, "I knew some sense had crept into you. Yes. What a great thought! And the suits will keep us warm... and... and.... they'll be one less thing we have to carry. That is an excellent idea!"

Within half an hour, they had packed, dressed in the hazmat suits, and were ready to go. They opened the bunker door, and, checking the area carefully, they proceeded out into the night.

\* \* \* \*

Calvin Rhodes climbed into the cab of the truck and put the key in the ignition. He turned it forward a bit and heard the slow, whining grind of the starter kick in, pumped the gas pedal slightly and felt the motor rumble to life.

Pulling out of the circular driveway, he waved to the small crowd of people standing at the foot of the porch, and then proceeded slowly along the gravel driveway, hearing the crunch of the tires underneath him, until he came to a stop where the driveway met the county highway. He looked both ways, although that wasn't really necessary. His was the only vehicle moving on the road. He pushed the knob forward, finding his gear, and gave the truck some gas. Cautiously, he drove the first ten feet of a journey that would take him halfway across the country, and, gently shifting gears, he settled his butt into the seat.

The first hundred miles were mostly uneventful. He stuck to the back roads, cruising through the rural scenery of the rolling hill country, passing family farms and churches and schools and small towns, or the burned out buildings that had once stood for them.

Mostly, there was an eerie quiet, although in some yards kids were still at play as their parents watched warily from the windows. In many places, the storefronts along streets were smashed, and the shelves were emptied, leaning over like dominoes one against another, tossed by looters or panicked citizens or both.

Coming to a stop at a rural junction, Calvin saw two corpses splayed out over the hood of a broken down car. Pockets were turned inside out, and the doors of the car stood wide open and the trunk was pulled up. The scene left little to the imagination, and it played before Calvin's eyes in seconds in blue-black flickers, and ended just as he saw it now, in tragedy.

He slowed just enough to hope for peace upon the souls of the victims and their families and to be grateful that it wasn't he.

The advantage to being in the country during this moment was the benefit of not having as many people to dodge. Statistically speaking, that was a very large advantage indeed. Calvin would drive along highway 79 almost as far as Memphis in order to avoid the Interstate highways, and he would pass, almost exclusively, through a few widely separated small towns—towns such as Hearne and Henderson and Carthage.

As he drove through the Piney Woods of Texas, he thought about all the places he'd seen and known and loved in the state. It was difficult for people who weren't from there to understand it... how Texas had plains, mountains, mighty rivers, and woods and forests, as well as deserts, and oceans... and skies. Plenty of skies. Of course, the state also had its large cities and its little towns, and that was what made it special for him—as a native Texan who was also an outsider of sorts. Texas didn't necessarily have the best *in anything*, but it had the best *of everything*. It was self-contained in a way that other places weren't. As the people often said, *Texas is a whole other country.* As he drove through the silent night, he looked up at the stars and saw that they were big and bright, and already he missed being deep in the state's heart.

Outside of Shreveport, he took gunfire. There was simply no other way around it. Shreveport, that is. The Louisiana city was a vexation that could not be avoided. Literally. He *had* to go through the town in order to reach the bridge that would take him over the Red River. The river, usually an afterthought, its muddy waters rolling lazily along as if the world and its affairs were none of its concern, had become a barrier that he needed to breach. Bridges, by nature, were bottlenecks, and danger always loves a bottleneck.

Calvin timed his approach so that he'd come to the crossing in the middle of the night. Winding his way south around the city, he came up to the bridge on $70^{th}$ Street, running adjacent to the old skeletal structures of Hamel's Amusement Park, which had closed down more than a decade ago when a tornado bent its Ferris Wheel in half.

He'd been thinking of the Ferris Wheel and comparing it in his mind to the recently destroyed one on Coney Island—the one from Hurricane Sandy— that he'd seen on the television and the internet just before those had gone black forever. He was driving alongside the amusement park looking out over the rusty machinery, the steel and wood standing alone in its abandoned memories, remembering how the recent world had simply stopped in the wake of Hurricane Sandy when, out of the blue—or the black, actually—he heard a ping. Then another.

The shots ricocheted off the fender of his pickup, and he swiveled his head to see where they were coming from. He almost ran off the bridge just as he entered its mouth.

Somewhere back at the amusement park, he thought. Not amusing at all.

He hit the gas, tore across the river, and looked up into his rear-view mirror to watch the rusted old skyline disappear into the night.

\* \* \* \*

"Why do you keep taking off your boots? Are you trying to slow us down?"

It was Val. He was standing over the round-faced man and sneering at him. The young man, Kent, peered into his boot and seemed to be searching for something that wasn't there. He was a little drunk. They'd taken turns watching through the night, and Kent had spent most of his turn sneaking drinks of vodka from a flask he'd kept secretly in his pocket. In his mind, his life had turned to dung and the vodka made it almost, but not quite, bearable.

"Leave him alone, Val. Just... don't start it up again." It was Steve. The silent one. Like his comrade Mike, he was getting tired of the constant bickering back and forth between Val and Kent, and he'd come to conclude that Val was mostly to blame. Val was like a rooster who, with nothing worthwhile at which to peck, pecked at anything near him that he deemed to be weaker than himself.

"Yes. Listen to our amigo, Esteban, here." Kent felt himself slurring his words. When he said 'Estaban,' it sounded to him like 'Esh-tra-gon.'

"Time's out of joint..." (He was speaking so slowly!) "No need to get your nose out of joint, too." The words came out like molasses, awkwardly, and ran together in his ears like they did not in his head.

The brutish Val looked at him as though someone getting his nose pushed out of joint was exactly what he desired. They were waiting for Mike to come back from a little hike up ahead to scout out their direction, and passing the time with Val was, as usual, not turning out to be rewarding for Kent, so he excused himself to walk over to a small group of bushes to let the vodka finish its pass through him.

"Stupid idiot," he muttered to himself as he half stumbled and half climbed up a small rise toward the bushes. "Of course, I'm trying to slow you down...," he slurred to himself. Walking over the rise, he stood at a small hedge line and was just about to unzip his pants when sobriety snuck up on him and a shot of adrenaline flew through his system like lightening... There, at the bottom of the hedges, in a small clump of trees, was a man dressed like an accountant. Blood, turned black and inky like impenetrable night, lay frozen in a pool around him.

* * * *

The man held up his hand for his friends to shut up. They were sitting in a group at the foot of the bridge where they'd been sitting for several days. Stalled cars and buses formed a zigzag maze designed to block access to the bridge from all vehicles, and to force pedestrians to walk... but only after paying a toll.

The friends had learned that it was easier to allow the food to come to them by standing with knives, boards, and chains across the bridge than it was to go out in search of it for themselves. Looting was turning out to be dangerous business in the city. The rumor was rampant that some looters had even been cooked and eaten. Charging tolls was much safer. They'd placed a sign on the off-ramp side of the bridge that told the people who were escaping out of the city that they needed to pay to cross—a fee for the right to exit hell. The gang told the citizens that the toll was something like an indulgence, and the gatekeepers, the popes and priests of the new order, administered punishments upon anyone who tried to exit without paying. The sign made it clear what forms of payment were acceptable...

*Weapons. Food. Money.*

It was unclear what they planned to do with the money.

"Hey. Shhh. Shhh. Shhhhhh."

They watched as a couple of yellow suits on what appeared to be bicycles came drifting down the decline. The bikes were taking their time, weaving slowly in and out of traffic and the suits riding the bikes turning their hooded heads first to this side and then to that side. The yellow suit in the lead seeming to point out little features on the ground to the suit in the back as they crept lazily, silently, eerily, through the deadened line of vehicles.

"What the...?" A man with a two by four with a few rusty nails protruding from the end was the one who couldn't quite find the last word he was searching for. He stood with the others, because all of them were standing now. As a group, they watched the yellow suits calmly apply the brakes on their bikes.

From a distance, maybe from the top of the bridge, one would have seen the tallest of the yellow suits dismount from the bike and calmly unstrap a pack tied to the back of the bicycle. The suit walked to the foot of the bridge, approached the circle of men, setting the bag slowly on the ground. From the height of the bridge, the yellow suit, looking something like an astronaut or a technician trying to control a viral outbreak, bent down, opened the bag, and began fishing around for something inside it. The other suit waited with the bikes. The men stood and stared with their weapons in anticipation...

In a movie, the music would have built to a crescendo, but this was not a movie. It was real life. When the yellow suit stood up with something strange in its hands, the men broke and ran. They scattered in all directions, running for cover like men chased by bees, or devils... or death. They never looked back.

With her head down, looking at the package in her hands, Veronica had missed the sight of the armed men fleeing in panic. Now, finding herself alone, she reached up and undid the helmet of her fallout suit and removed it and felt the cold air slip across her face. She opened the box of graham crackers she held in her hands and carefully tore open the interior packaging. Removing a cracker, she took a bite. She slipped the cardboard flap back in its slot and dropped the box back in the bag, and, throwing the bag across her shoulders, she walked back to Stephen.

"What was that about, mom?"

"I guess they weren't hungry," Veronica said.

She put her helmet back on and mounted her bike, and she and Stephen rode down into the highway leading into Staten Island.

# Chapter 11
# Contact

The man struggled gamely, but he was stuck fast. He'd fallen through the boards of the dilapidated bridge, and the wood had given way just enough to bite into his leg but not enough to allow it to wriggle free. He didn't have the leverage or the angle to pull his leg out. He was looking at the leg as if deep in thought, perhaps determining whether he had other choices. He ran his hand along the back of his neck and then over a few day's growth of beard.

Hidden in the trees, Lang could see that the man's ankle had become wedged in the supporting cross braces of the old footbridge, and that he was unable to reach down through the broken boards to free himself no matter what he tried.

Peter watched along with the others as the man struggled, and he noted aloud that the man had better find a way to get loose. "If he doesn't manage to free himself, he's surely going to die..." Peter paused. "...if not from the injury or starvation, then from some group of troublesome passersby looking for gear, guns, or just trouble. They'll eventually come upon him."

"We need to help him," Lang told Peter, looking at the older man with a face that betrayed both fear and compassion.

"I don't know, Lang," Peter said. He stared, unblinking at the man on the bridge. He could not help but see both the metaphor... the bridge itself... and the danger. "Helping him could put us all at risk. We could be found ou—"

"Oh, for heaven's sake, Peter!" Natasha snapped, interrupting him. "What if that was you stuck there on that bridge?"

"Well," Peter said, "sure... I would want someone to help me... but I'd also not expect it. I'd understand if they couldn't do it without great risk to themselves."

"Still, I'd like to go and check on him, Peter," Lang said.

"You can't go, Lang." The old man looked at the youth, his skin pale and beginning to look almost transparent. "You can't even lift your arm up! How are you going to help this man get free with one arm?" Peter paused, staring at Lang. Then he looked down for a beat before adding, "No... If anyone is going, I'm going."

"Peter, be reasonable," Lang said. "Who's going to protect Natasha and Elsie if you get shot out there? It has to be me. I'll go."

The two men continued their argument, and as they did, Natasha's eyes grew wide, and she knelt down as if she needed to inspect her boot. She looked up, then left and then right, and before either Lang or Peter could say anything to stop her, she was sprinting full speed towards the bridge. She stayed low to the ground, maintaining maximum cover as she ran...

Her actions caused the others to stop in their tracks, and spring into action. Without a word, Peter raised the rifle and balanced the barrel on the small branch just to his left. He adjusted the iron sights, allowed a bit for windage and the expected drop, and began to steady his breath, willing himself to slow his heartbeat.

*If this man makes a wrong move*, Peter thought... *I'll drop him.*

Without taking his eye away from the sights, Peter whispered to Lang, who was mentally already on his way, leaning in anticipation, to take the .22 Marlin and run to the low hill to the northeast.

"Stay under cover," Peter raised his voice. "That gun is good, as-is, from seventy-five to one hundred meters. Keep your eyes on the woods and watch the dirt road as it comes around that bend. If anyone, anyone at all approaches..." He let the implications hang in the air and whispered quietly under his breath, to himself as much as to Lang, "Don't miss."

\* \* \* \*

Natasha reached the old, decrepit bridge, and the man finally saw her. He slowly lowered his right hand, moving as if he were testing her, determining whether she was going to ask him to stop... and she saw that he had a Glock pistol strapped to his good leg.

"Wait!" Natasha shouted, with authority. "Don't do it! If you move, and your hand gets near that gun, your head will explode. Trust me. You are in the sights of someone who is very, very good. Just... please... don't be stupid. I'm here to help you, and I'm unarmed."

She turned around slowly with her hands up, and lifted her coat so that he could see she did not have a gun of her own.

The man stared at Natasha for a second. Without blinking, without giving any indication on his face of his thinking one way or the other about anything, his hand opened up very slowly, and swiveled at the wrist to show whoever she was talking about... whoever was pointing a gun at him... that he had no intention of doing anything stupid. Methodically, he put both hands flat down on the wood surface of the bridge, and then paused, just staring at Natasha without a word.

"That's good. I see you are clever," Natasha said, moving again toward the man. "I'm going to climb under the bridge and see if I can get your ankle free. If I were you, even if it hurts horribly and you want to scream out, I wouldn't move very much, or make any noise."

The man didn't respond at all. He just answered with his eyes, a slow blink that declared openly and plainly that he understood what this woman and her people expected of him. That he'd been given a kind of trust...

With that, Natasha hurried down the embankment, and, near the edge of the tiny stream, she climbed upward into the ancient trusses and supports that held the weight of the old bridge.

\* \* \* \*

Ten minutes later, they were sitting in the cover of trees. Peter worked on the quiet man's ankle, examining it to determine if it was broken or if there was any serious injury. Just a moment ago, Natasha and the quiet man had come hobbling in together. Drawing close to Peter's location, Natasha ran ahead to get the medical bag, before remembering that they no longer had it. Happily, there was no need for it; the man's ankle wasn't in any serious danger.

"It'll be sore awhile, and if we were in the old world I'd tell you to stay off of it and take it easy, but obviously you can't do that now." Peter looked at the others and wondered if they remembered what it was like to be back in that other life, then he looked back to the man to see if he gave any indication of his thinking, but he did not.

Peter turned to Lang, "I don't even know if he speaks English or if he understands me. Perhaps he is a mute." He raised his voice to the man, speaking slowly, "Do you understand?"

"He speaks English," Lang said with a slight smirk on his face. "And he understands you. At least, he understood Natasha well enough, back at that bridge..."

"People communicate in many ways," Peter said, "some body language conveys as much understanding as words."

Natasha nodded her agreement to Lang's opinion. "He understood the words I said. Apparently, he's just the quiet type."

The quiet man—about twenty years old, handsome and well built, with blue eyes and sandy-colored hair—looked slowly over to Lang and smiled without saying a word.

"Well, there's not much I can say for his gifts of conversation," Peter said. He helped the man re-lace his boot and then stand to his feet. The man gave a little hop as he did so. The ankle was tentative, at best, but he applied weight to it and then stood up straight, as if to indicate that the injury was not going to be a problem for him.

The man was dressed in what had once been an army green coat and BDU pants, but the man had engaged in some makeshift winter camouflage attempts, and the coat and pants had been hastily spray painted with splotches of white paint, and here and there outlines of green pine branches appeared among the white patches.

His gun, a bolt-action sniper rifle with a pricey scope attached to it, he'd camouflaged with white and green as well. His backpack matched the rest of him.

Peter nodded to the man, and then to the weapons each of them carried, as if he was bringing attention to the fact that he was not going to cause anyone trouble, and he didn't want any in return.

"Well, sir," Peter said, "I don't know who you are or where you came from... or what you're doing out here..." He glanced at the man. "We don't know whose side you're on, or if you are a good guy or a bad guy, but—"

"It's okay," the man said quietly. It was the first words he'd spoken. "It's really... it is best..." The four others stared at him, and he shook his head that he meant it. He wanted the older man to understand that he appreciated the hospitality, but he understood that the group now had to be on their way.

"We should just part and wish each other well," the man said.

Then, the awkward moment was over, and the man just stared at Peter without any hint of a response on his face.

"Well... sir... you are free to travel with us," Peter told him, in case that might influence his decision. "We're short-handed and under-trained, but we could use the extra gun and skills. Up to a point. It's up to you."

The man shook his head no, and he picked up the rifle and tossed it over his shoulder by the strap before doing the same with his bag over the other shoulder. He turned to walk away, limping only slightly on his injured ankle. Just as he was about to disappear into the thick brush of the woods, he turned and looked at all four of the travelers, one at a time...

"Ace," he said, matter-of-factly and without any apparent emotion. "That's my name," he said. "And... thank you all." He acted as if that was all that needed to be said.

Ace then turned back toward the woods, and with a few confident steps, he was gone.

Lang looked at Natasha and Elsie and noticed that they sat there staring for a few extra beats, watching as Ace disappeared into the woods. Ace was a good-looking man, no denying it, Lang thought. He didn't blame the ladies for being a bit taken with him. A smile broke across his face. He shook his head, and they all stared at each other for a moment, searching to see if everyone was having the same thoughts about the strange encounter with this man... and then they all broke into laughter.

\* \* \* \*

They came upon the abandoned cabin just as darkness began to fall. Some kind of violence had occurred there, though there were no corpses evident lying around the place. They could tell there had been violence by the pockmarking of bullet holes in the walls, and the telltale signs that looters or bandits or... maybe just regular folks had ransacked the place. The door hung loosely on the hinges, and the glass from most of the windows was lying shattered on the ground instead of safely in its frames.

We know the events that we experience, and we have some knowledge of the legends that we are told, but the mind reels at the stories a place like this could tell when the world as we know it has ended. This lonely cabin in the woods had seen numerous such tales play out as individuals, groups, and bandits, and maybe even armies had crisscrossed these woods in search of some place "safe." The story of our four travelers was just now intersecting with this cabin... but dozens of other stories, all of them just as important to the characters living through them, had unfolded here. From the looks of the place, not all of them had ended well.

"Buildings make me nervous," Peter said. "We don't have enough people to secure a building, for one thing..." He paused, as if there were no reason number two. "It is shelter, sure, but it's not much more than that." He looked around at the place and considered the things that to him were painfully apparent, if one only cared to look. "If we stay too long, more people will be coming along."

"Lang has to rest, Peter," Natasha said. Elsie nodded her head in agreement and added, "And his wound needs treatment. He's growing weaker, and the pain is obvious on his face." Natasha touched Peter on the arm, and gave him a little smile, "We need to stop."

They went through the building thoroughly, checking every place where someone might be hiding, but they found no one. Then they began to prepare an area to treat Lang's wound. Peter briefed the women on what they would need to do, which didn't take long seeing that their meds and first aid case had been stolen.

He patted Lang lightly on the back, then told Natasha, who'd been standing lookout at the door, that he needed go up front and secure the premises.

"You guide Elsie through the steps that I taught you. Do it thoroughly, and call me if you need anything."

Elsie helped Lang remove his shirt, and it became clear, very quickly, that things were not right. The skin was pale and the area on the arm surrounding the wound was angry, red, and warm to the touch. The gunshot wound was infected, and it was much worse than they'd suspected.

The darkness was starting to invade the cabin. Natasha called to Peter who came down the hall, and, as he did, she stepped out into the hallway to meet him. Peter knew that if there were anything at all that they could do to help Lang, they'd have to do it quickly, before the cabin became shrouded in darkness. *He might not survive another day if we don't do something now,* Peter thought, *the world itself might become shrouded in darkness.*

*Something must be done. But what?*

\* \* \* \*

Clive Darling guided the rigged-up RV he called *Bernice* up a small incline until he could just see Carbondale over the bulge of the dashboard. The black, armored chase vehicles that accompanied him split up as he brought Bernice to a stop. Some moved to his left and others to his right. They moved in a line, the vehicles, until they came to a stop, like sentries out on a search, an ancient tribal ritual played out in modern sleek machinery. Doors and hatches on the vehicles opened up with precision, and soldiers poured forth from them, and in seconds the team had set up a secure perimeter, which included snipers and patrols.

Clive turned to his passenger and explained that he'd learned that the maniac running the Carbondale "resettlement" center had secured generators and a power plant. Clive explained that the officer running the prison camp was planning on electrifying the fences and illuminating the control tents where interrogations were said to be taking place around the clock.

The listener listened. He watched the man speak with confidence about how a life ought to be lived. He heard in that voice, the voice of the man named Clive, the intonations and ideas of a brother.

As Clive spoke, the listener saw a man who knew what he was about. Clive's mannerisms showed the listener that the man with the Savannah drawl really believed the words that he said, and that he was not full of guile. This made the listener think of his own journey, his own modern ride, his own tribal ties...

"They don't need electrical power to terrorize the public," Clive said to the passenger, his slow drawl emphasizing the horror in the word... *Terrorize.*

Clive indicated with his hand the general world... first the world outside... then the world inside... over there in Carbondale. "They seem to have been doin'..." He paused. "...you know... the terrorizing... alright by themselves. But—"

Clive paused and looked at his passenger, the man so odd in his own weird skin, this man who seemed to mold himself around the world, and yet, who in the end molded the world around him... He watched his passenger listening, as they sat in the RV with their soldiers spread out in a perimeter around them. As they waited, the two men just passed time... just sharing... like friends would.

The friends noticed when the power blinked on in the Carbondale camp, first with some hesitation... and then more insistently.

The lights pierced the surrounding darkness.

* * * *

But not everywhere, though... the lights only burned in the tents of arbitrary power.

\* \* \* \*

Clive massaged his heavy mustache with his left hand and looked over to his passenger. He indicated to the broader world again, and when he did, his passenger listened.

"There's no way we can insure fairness in this world... and even if we could, I don't think I'd want to. People are not equal, and no one can make them what they are not... However, the use of arbitrary power in the hands of tyranny perturbs me. We Luddites look to impair, obstinately, such terrorism where we find it."

Clive looked at his passenger... his passenger looked at him.

"My friend... would you like to do the honors?"

The red-bearded passenger smiled, and his eyes lit up.

Clive lifted up the protective guard on the dashboard, exposing the lighted switch.

\* \* \* \*

In the Carbondale Resettlement Camp, the technician had just finished a long day of fixing, and prepping, and wiring, and fueling up the huge generators. He pulled down the three large levers that would connect the machines to the makeshift "grid" in the camp. After running through a series of checks, the technician flipped up a plastic button guard, and then pressed in the red button with his thumb.

The generators fired up in unison, and the technician was pleased to see the lights in the maintenance tent first flicker, and then begin to burn brightly through the plastic windows.

He'd just packed up his tools and was rushing back to the tent to get out of the cold, when he heard the loud rumble accompanied with the otherworldly buzz.

The buzz was otherworldly.

Earthshaking and otherworldly.

It seemed that there was a split-second of silence before the entire control panel and junction box on the front of each of the generators blew up, showering pieces of metal and wire around the camp like rain.

The technician ran quickly along the packed white snow as the electrical sparks shot out in in white arcs above his head...

From a distance it might have looked like an umbrella, or a fireworks show.

On the other hand, maybe it looked like a mushroom cloud.

It was hard to tell. The artificial light was so brief. And so rare.

\* \* \* \*

The red-bearded man smiled when the lights went dark again in the camp.

"I sing the body electric. I celebrate the me... yet... to come!"

He looked at Clive, who smiled at him under his thick mustache. "It's almost like bein' the Good Lord there for a few seconds," he said with a wink, his eyes wide, like a child's.

He sat there, Clive did, and looked over the dash to the darkened prison camp that was Carbondale, Pennsylvania.

"Insufficient shielding," Clive Darling said, matter-of-factly. "We tried to warn 'em."

# Chapter 12
# Blood

Natasha did her best not to show concern on her face, and she smiled stiffly, but she was worried. They were in the middle of nowhere with no antibiotics, no herbal remedies, not even any natural antibiotics like garlic, Echinacea, or even honey. She'd instructed Elsie to start a fire in the fireplace to boil some water, while she went to find Peter to determine what she might do next to prepare, aid, and support whatever treatment Lang might need.

She found him moving stealthily towards the tree line behind the cabin, catching up with him with a low shout. "The wound is infected, Peter," she said, "and I don't think just cleaning it and repacking it is going to do anything but cause him excruciating pain. You're going to have to come and help."

Peter grimaced. The last gray-blue of the gloaming was highlighting the trees, and a cold wind began to whip through them, making the shadows move across the snowy ground.

He was concerned about Lang, and he saw fear and nervousness etched across Natasha's face.

"Absolutely..."

Peter's mind was torn. He was also concerned with security. Lang was his friend, and was like a son to him, but with the four of them all inside the house, they'd be blind, and exposed. He wasn't happy about that. Security was really everything right now. If only the women could deal with Lang...

He didn't know what he might do with the wound that the women could not either. He wasn't sure there was anything to *be* done at all.

Still, he had to do *something* to help Lang or the boy wouldn't last long. Sepsis was a concern, and there wasn't anything he could think of at that moment that frightened him more than that. If the infection got into the blood stream... well... he'd just have to see if there was anything he could do.

\* \* \* \*

Walking back into the cabin, Peter had no idea what he should do about Lang. Absent a medical solution—and he had to admit that his own library of knowledge and experience had already been taxed to its limit—there wasn't much left he could do.

The rudiments of an extravagant *placebo* plan had run through his mind when he first noticed that Lang was getting worse. Convincing someone that a medicine or a procedure is effectual—when in reality it was not—can be very powerful, not just in convincing the injured or sick person that they are getting better, but often enough that the positive effects of a placebo extend to actual physiological healing. The body, convinced that something powerful or helpful is going on, will often ramp up its own defenses to match or meet the expected results. In this way, patients have had their pain alleviated during surgery and recovery, and there were even cases of people healed of cancers and other real diseases with the use of placebos alone.

In his own mind, Peter called his plan "The Sugar Pill Plot." Placebos were often just sugar pills, made to look like the real thing. In tests, doctors or scientists gave sugar pills to some subjects while others received real medications. Often, those who received the sugar pills responded to the treatment as positively as those who had received the real medicine.

The mind is a powerful thing. Peter knew that, and, without any other solution, he was contemplating a very involved ruse as a last ditch way to try to help Lang.

He felt in his pocket and noticed that he still had the cell phone from the man he'd been forced to shoot. Peter knew that cell phones were loaded with trace amounts of gold and silver, and that both gold and silver have been used for millennia as antibiotics and antivirals. He also knew that he didn't have the proper tools, chemicals, or equipment to extract the gold and silver from the phone... *but*, he thought to himself, and this was the thing... *Lang doesn't know that.*

The first thing Peter did was to gather Natasha and Elsie together. He told them that the three of them needed to black out the windows. They were going to have fire and light in the cabin, and they wanted as little evidence of that to be evident from outside the cabin as possible. The smoke from the fireplace was bad enough. Peter thought that he should have asked them not to light a fire in the first place; however, since they'd already started the fire, he would use it to sterilize the knife and prepare his placebo ruse.

Using the flashlight for light, Peter proceeded to cut large squares of carpet from the floor of the cabin and instructed Natasha and Elsie to find nails, staples, or any other materials that might be useful for hanging the squares. He told them that they could fasten them over the windows by pounding bent and rusted nails through the carpet and into the window frames using a brick and a rock they'd found behind the cabin. It took 45 minutes for the water to boil sufficiently for Peter to get to work.

He started by taking the phone apart. He made a big show of the disassembly process. In his mind he noted that he was not only *disassembling*, but he was also *dissembling*... which meant lying. It was good that the trick was a secret, because he didn't know how poorly his word play might be received at such a time.

He removed the chip, the processor, wires, and connector from the phone, all the while announcing loudly and confidently everything that he was doing. He convinced himself of the lie, so that his patient might more readily believe him. He gave a short dissertation on the antibiotic, antiviral, and anti-bacterial benefits of silver and gold in solution. *All that part was true*, he thought. He worked like a magician, using sleight of hand and showmanship to make the whole display believable. Nobody doubted him. He noted that he was manipulating the trust of his friends, *but–* He forced the thought to leave him. He didn't have time for self-recrimination.

"Natasha? Elsie? Have you finished blacking out the cabin?" Peter called out from down the hallway.

"Yes, Peter. It's all done," Natasha replied.

"Okay, while I finish this, I want you two to do a top to bottom search of this place. Examine every cabinet, drawer, cubbyhole, shelf... *everywhere*... Anything you find, call it out loudly... OK?

"You holler out what it is to me, and I'll tell you if we can use it. There's probably not much to be found. The place looks like it's been stripped bare, but you never know..."

He stepped back into the room and then stuck his head into the hallway again, as an afterthought, choosing to err on the side of caution... "Stay away from any windows," he warned. "Even brushing up against one can cause a disturbance that might be seen from outside."

The two women called out agreement and began their search. Peter used the momentary diversion to pour out the solution he'd been concocting. He filled an empty coffee cup with water from one of his water bottles, then added a tiny pinch off of the ChapStick to the water. His plan was to heat the water in the cup by the fire so that it would melt the tiny amount of ChapStick. The oily substance would add a peculiar taste that Peter hoped would amplify the placebo effect on Lang's mind.

\* \* \* \*

"An old aluminum soda can!" Elsie shouted from one of the bedrooms.

"Keep it!" Peter responded.

"An empty Bourbon bottle!" Natasha yelled, even though she was just fifteen feet away in the little kitchen nook, searching through the cabinets.

"Keep it!" Peter yelled back, laughing.

"A knitting needle!" Elsie hollered.

"Keep it!" Peter and Lang shouted back, in unison.

Lang was now laughing through the pain, and the diversion was good for him. "This place is a veritable treasure trove of valuable artifacts," he said. He was surprised that there were so many useful things still available in the cabin—items most people would probably think were useless.

Peter took the hot coffee cup away from the fire and allowed it to cool for thirty seconds or so. Then he handed it to Lang and told him to drink it all down.

"Swallow it to the dregs, son. That concoction will make you right as rain."

Lang did what he was told and scowled a bit from the strange oiliness in the water.

"A quarter bag of sugar!" Natasha yelled.

"Keep it!" Lang shouted, chuckling at the game.

"Woah! Wait!" Peter said. "Did you say *sugar*, Natasha?"

"Yes, Peter. Refined sugar. Kind of clumpy, but still white."

"Oh my goodness," Peter said, and excitement lit up his features. "Bring it here, daughter. You may just be a lifesaver!"

Natasha walked over by the fire with the bag of sugar. "Why?" she asked. "What good is sugar? Are we going to eat it?"

"Well, young lady. Refined and bleached sugar has a multitude of excellent uses, but eating it is *not* one of them. In fact, one of the poorest uses of refined sugar is as a food substance. It has killed more humans than Stalin and Mao combined." He paused, winking at Lang, as if to say... *it's true...* then he continued. "But it is good for many medicinal reasons, not the least of which is the fact that sugar and honey have been used as an antibacterial agent for millennia..." The older man began to elucidate on the healing properties of sugar but, at that moment, Natasha and Lang were not entirely paying attention. They were looking at one another.

When Natasha had entered the room with the bag of sugar, she'd glanced sideways at Lang. They caught one another's attention and held the look for what was a tiny moment that seemed like much longer to each of them. The glance was a tiny visual embrace, but then they released it and smiled to one another, as if to say... *There he goes again.*

\* \* \* \*


## Monday

No one got much sleep. Treating Lang's infected wound stretched into the wee hours of the morning, and it had been a soul-wrenching mind siege, every single minute of it.

Before Natasha found the sugar, Peter hadn't had much hope left at all. The placebo trick wasn't real or tangible, but, at the time, it was the only real hope he had of halting or reversing Lang's infection.

The boy had been valiant. He had not even complained, not once, though Peter knew that he was in severe pain. In the older man's mind, finding the sugar had been a miracle. He'd exhausted his knowledge and experience, and, without just such a miracle, a stupid mind game was all that he had remaining in his bag of tricks.

Peter wasn't sure how far to take the whole miracle thing. *Even if we had the strongest antibiotics... nothing can guarantee success*, Peter thought. He grimaced, thinking that such was always the case. There were never any guarantees. Perfectly healthy people were dying by the thousands and tens of thousands every day.

He recalled the story of a group of people who had rescued a young, injured seal. They worked hard and nursed the seal back to health, and on a glorious day under a bright, blue sky they released the seal back into the wild with great fanfare, only to have the seal eaten by a huge shark within seconds of being set free. Life is tenuous. Peter knew that. Even when everything goes right, it is tenuous. He wasn't deceived about the probabilities of any of them living through the next year. *My dear uncle*, he thought... Peter recalled his uncle Volkhov, and smiled when he considered what Lev would have thought of this young man who was being so brave. He wondered, grimly, whether his uncle would turn out to be right... if he'd been correct when he'd predicted that more than 90% of the population would die within a year.

Locating the sugar changed everything. Sugar, indeed, was one of the most effective natural treatments for infection known to man. This was no tall tale or attempt at alchemic voodoo. The problem is that, in order to apply the sugar remedy properly, the wound had to be opened, debrided and prepared. That meant that, due to the pain and sensitivity caused by the infection, Peter had been forced to subject Lang to a torturous several hours of the most excruciating pain that either one of them could have ever imagined.

Using the knife from Lang's pack, sterilized and wielded somewhat clumsily by a man who was knowledgeable and wise, if not practiced and efficient, Peter had removed all of the dead and infected flesh, some of it already turning gangrenous and rotting into the wound. The process was slow and exceedingly painful.

The debridement, which entailed the physical removal of all dead and infected material from the wound, was difficult, and Lang had to suffer through it without any anesthesia. They didn't even have the vodka. That had been in Peter's backpack when it was stolen. All they had now was the leather sheath, and Lang had endured the torture admirably.

After cleaning and debriding the bullet hole (on both sides), a waiting period ensued while the wound bled a bit, and then they waited until that blood seepage stopped and coagulation had begun. Peter then packed the wound with the processed white sugar, which would act much as it does when it is used as a preservative on meat, blending with the blood and juices to create a thick "syrup" that then caused osmotic shock to the cells in the wound.

Peter explained this all to Natasha as he performed the treatment.

Elsie also sat and listened, taking notes in case she ever needed to remember how to do this. Taking notes also helped Elsie keep her mind off of the pain that Lang was evidently suffering.

Peter spoke on. "Osmotic shock means that the cells will give up their moisture and basically become de-hydrated. This will rob the infection and bacteria of oxygen and water needed to spread and grow..." He raised his hands, as if making a choking motion.

"Sugar has been used to treat serious battle wounds for centuries, and, even in the $21^{st}$ Century, some doctors and experts had come to believe that it should be the primary means of treating bullet wounds and subsequent infections."

Peter and his lectures, Natasha thought for a split second... She looked at Lang but he did not meet her gaze. He seemed to be too weak to show her any interest.

* * * *

Hours later, Lang rested comfortably, and the women were off talking in one of the other rooms of the cabin.

Peter ruminated on one of those odd little coincidences in life. Really, and truly, they have no real reason to exist. And yet they do, those moments of perfect beauty.

At that very moment, Peter was standing guard over his flock like a mother goose, or a father goose. He was thinking about the usefulness of the sugar. And he was thinking how that such knowledge... so much of it... is lost on the new generations. Then again, he also realized that he did not know as much—it had to be admitted—as his Uncle Lev. *So many people*, Peter thought, *do not know or value what they have right there in front of them...* if only they had eyes to see...

Now, he was packing and repacking the backpack, while mentally sorting through the small little disturbances in his system. He needed to maintain a tightly catalogued system to know what they had and what they lacked.

And he came across a small blue box.

The box was in the backpack that had belonged to the man named Clay.

He looked at the box.

He held it up and wondered what was in it. He'd said he would open it if ever there was a moment when the contents might be used to help them survive or to save a life. He'd not thought of the box when he'd almost given up on treating Lang with anything other than a parlor trick.

Peter did wonder if anything in the box could speak to the issue, but, just in the nick of too late, the sugar had come to the rescue, and now he felt like the sanctity of the box must remain intact. He could not have explained *why,* if you'd asked him to, but he trusted his gut. He placed the box back in the bag, sat, and thought.

Altogether, for Peter, it was a moment of perfect beauty, the placing of the sugar in the wound, and then the box in the bag. Like in some, perhaps even many, of our best moments, there was an unknown connection, something tangible but also spiritual. He felt that there was a connection in the confluence of events that was unknown because unknowable. There was something in *not* looking in the blue box, because that box had a purpose, and that purpose was *not yet.* If Natasha had not found the sugar, and then Peter had been searching the backpack, he'd surely have opened the box. But Natasha had found the sugar, and it was perfect. It was what was needful at the moment.

Sure. He'd be disappointed if, upon opening the box someday, it turned out that the box was full of childhood teeth, or Chiclet gum, or beads from some bracelet or necklace from long ago. That would be a downer, for certain, because Peter believed that whatever was in that box was important. It was for saving lives. It had to be. It was for the sustenance of that crucial belief that he once again refused to open the blue box. This once... this one shining moment... Peter trusted his gut.

\* \* \* \*

As the darkness gave way to gray, and then the gray succumbed to the brightness of the new morning, three of the travelers slept a little longer than they should have, and the fourth... Peter... hadn't slept at all. He'd tried to maintain watch but had drifted in and out of deeper and deeper thought... anything to keep his mind off of Lang...

For this reason, none of them were ready when the attack came.

It all started peacefully enough. Peter, eyes open, was slipping in and out of brain sleep as he leaned against a tree. He'd been looking down at the cabin from a small ridge to the southwest of the structure when some men rode up on horseback and said hello.

He never saw them or heard them coming.

# Chapter 13
# Stream

Life often goes along in a stream. The details float by like a leaf on a river. The current is pushing and pulling the leaf, but we do not see it because we are standing on the banks of the river, attending to our lives. There are moments when the leaf is caught up in little eddies. Events pile up. They gather like twigs—like flotsam and jetsam—caught up in the stream of life. Time blocks and unblocks in little bursts at such places. Information pours through like water. The details crystallize. Various pressures and turbulences in the river, pouring into the sea of life, push and pull, but we do not see it. We do not see the leaf *or* the pushing and pulling.

Because we are standing on the banks, attending to our lives.

The leaf cannot be blamed for our missing it. Nor, from its perspective, should it care that we missed it. For its part, it is merely floating down the river on its back, caught up in swirling little curlicues of water, looking up at the stars.

Perhaps, in the end, it is a matter of perspective after all. Perhaps if the leaf were to notice us, standing there on the shore... *we* would seem like mere details. Perhaps the leaf would think that *we* are just details among many other details... standing there along the banks... trying to be seen or to avoid being seen.

But sometimes even that is not the case.

*Sometimes we are the leaf.*

We get caught up in ourselves, in our own bodies, or in the stream. We are running, or driving, or riding... but almost always we are in motion. The details, the narrative flow of our lives, the events... they simply stream along past us. Drawing from the past... pushing toward an unknown future.

Perhaps we can be blamed for what we miss, we who are in perpetual movement. Perhaps not. We feel the miles roll by underneath us on the highway and feel them to be, like the stars overhead, endless, when they are not. We drift along on those details, noticing them as if they were standing on the river waving to us as we stream along. But we do not really notice them... the details... not *really*. Because we are on automatic pilot, just lazily floating down the river.

This happens even in catastrophes. We miss the signs.

\* \* \* \*

It was almost midnight, and Veronica and Stephen had covered an incredible amount of ground on their bikes in two straight days of riding.

They'd ridden across Staten Island, and then into New Jersey, and on into Pennsylvania. If you had asked Veronica to tell you her plan—what she hoped to do—she would simply have pointed to the ground and said... "Get as far away from *here* as possible."

After crossing the Verrazano Bridge, they'd passed through the destruction of the storm called Sandy on Staten Island. There were still boats in people's yards, some sitting on roofs of houses, and rubble and debris were everywhere. The Island was all covered with snow now. Here and there, the rubble peeked up through the piles of snow, as if to remind the people that it—the rubble—was still there.

Veronica and Stephen rode along through the broken city and past the destruction, past the piles of snow. Here and there they dodged rats that skittered across their pathway. Their hazmat gear barely raised an eyebrow as they rode along the coastline, and they rode on through the frozen fog likes ghosts, their yellow suits shimmering with a light glistening with moist sea air.

They rode past the piles of broken boards, the twisted pieces of siding, the musty old couches... all frozen under snow piled high along the rubble's edges in heaping white mounds. They passed by in silence.

They passed into New Jersey and into the suburbs and crossed bridges and hills and streams. They pushed forward like pilgrims, seeking a celestial city... or at the very least, a better country.

\* \* \* \*

Closer to the cities, the people were fleeing. The crowds were fleeing. They were on the bridges and the byways. They pushed like cattle through a chute where the roads narrowed around the debris of cars and trucks strewn through the streets. Vehicles and obstacles caused the waters of humanity to bulge around them like boulders in a stream, and, at the overpasses, the humans would stack up and bubble and roil until the waters made their way to the narrowed passage where they would gain speed and pick up momentum before shooting out of the other side. The people streamed along as if they were being drawn out of the cities and into the countryside by gravity or some other force of physics. They all walked with purpose, heading... *Where?*

\* \* \* \*

Veronica and Stephen had passed through the crowd as if in a protective bubble. Their hazmat suits worked like talismans. The crowds opened up around them as if they had the plague, as if they were aliens just landed on earth, and no one wanted to get too close.

Veronica and Stephen traveled as if under a star.

As darkness began to fall, the crowds thinned. Then, eventually, they disappeared altogether.

It was almost midnight.

Veronica and Stephen rode their bikes along the back country roads that spread across the Pennsylvania countryside like a capillary system, drawing the goods from the richest farms in the world to market.

Every once in a while, they would get off the bikes and walk them for a spell. Or, they would stand and rest for a few moments and look at their surroundings in excitement and wonder.

"These roads once all led to Hershey," Veronica said. She pointed off in the distance to a skyline that was darkened except for what was illuminated by the moon.

Stephen smacked his lips. "Man! If *I* only had a Reese's cup right about now!" He poked her in the ribs.

"Naughty boy. One day, I will show you your Gramam's recipe for chocolate. It is twice as good..."

Stephen just laughed and they stood with their bikes and looked down the fence lines at the farms along the road.

"They are among the most productive in the world... and the most beautiful..." She indicated with her hand to the farms. "...and see how the fields spread thick with snow in wide white blankets?" She pointed with her hand to the thick white swatches of color in front of them. "They look like *that* most winters. The snow lies there and replenishes the earth. And in spring they turn the pig manure under. Ewww." She waved her hand in front of her nose. "Then the whole county stinks... but it's not so bad when they use horse or cow dung."

"How do you know all this, mom?"

"I learned how to read, boy. You should too." She looked at him sideways. "You with your video games..." They shared a look and remembered where they were... and what the world was like now.

It wasn't really hard to do, the remembering, standing there, as they were, in the midst of the wide blue world, the ancient winter of Pennsylvania farmland rising up around them in a glow, their bright yellow suits shimmering in the moonlight.

\* \* \* \*

"Dude, I saw this interview with Manson once. He said the difference between him and the regular people out there is that..." The tattooed teenager paused and leaned forward. "Give me a loosie." The other young man handed him a cigarette. He lit his match and fired up the end, and then he indicated to the world with the cigarette. "If the regular guy out there... if he stepped off a bus in Des Moines at 10 p.m. and called his Aunt Gertrude and she wasn't home." The tattooed young fellow blew out smoke in tiny little circles, and coughed. "And Aunt Gertrude was his only ride. And if he was flat broke... The average guy wouldn't know what to do with himself. Whereas he... Manson... would dip into an alley and grab a tire iron and he'd be in business."

*Snort. Hmph!* The second young man, who was listening to the tattooed young fellow rattle, gave only this harrumphing series of audible gesticulations as retort, and this conversation continued thusly for a while.

The two teens were sitting by the roadside, crouched low to the ground in a ditch. They were part of a militia patrol unit sent forward to scope out the road. Actually, they were scouts for a group of bandits, but they liked to think of themselves as a militia. They'd copped some uniforms, and several of the older bandits had military experience, so they'd received a little training, but not much. They called themselves the *Pennsylvania Anarchists Corp*, the PAC, or usually, "The PACK."

This unit, made up almost entirely of new recruits, orphans, and people forced into duty by the leaders, had been sent forward to make sure the road was safe, but right now the boys were sitting along a ditch. Actually, to be accurate, they were sitting *in* the ditch and telling stories to one another—trying to impress each other with their toughness, their readiness to do whatever it takes—the way teenaged boys will.

They didn't notice at first when the two yellow suits rode up on bikes.

\* \* \* \*

*Sometimes life can go by like a stream of details in a narrative. Page after page, the stream of time pushes through, gathering force. The details can be like brushwork on a painting, the build up of the paint. Or like the fingers at the keyboard, the wastebasket full of crumpled ideas. The drink of scotch, the scratch of a head, the scratching out of ideas on pads of paper. The pushing in of soil around the roots. The coming of spring. All this is done in the pursuit of art. Beauty, and Art. Which are to enliven and protect life. Because the point of all this... the point of all this... is to enliven and protect life. To live, that is, in the here and the now. To live thoroughly and authentically. To live in nature. To walk out under the stars like Whitman and look up in the silence and take it all in.*

Veronica was thinking these things as they pedaled along.

*It is really very simple,* Veronica thought. *The point is to live–and to keep living.*

*Hear that,* she told herself.

The point is... *to live.*

\* \* \* \*

Veronica and Stephen were riding their bikes along. They had no idea what they were riding into because all they could see was white and even more white. Patches of field spread out across them in the moonlight, lying out across the country with its breathless picture-like series of farms and fields. It looked like an Amish quilt. The fields of white were intercut with black segmenting lines that ran their way around the edges of the farms. Veronica and Stephen were simply riding along enjoying the cool night air, weaving down another mile of long thin ribbon.

At first Veronica didn't even see him. The man simply stepped out into the roadway and held up his hand. It was probably his rifle she saw first. Slung across his shoulder the way it was, it hung at a right angle to his body, intersecting his torso, pointing up at right angles to the nighttime sky. She had just begun to focus on the rifle when she felt herself motioning to Stephen to stop. She began to search for the pistol she had strapped to her bike.

That's when a gang of bandits descended on them from all sides.

\* \* \* \*

Calvin Rhodes also cruised along the stream of time. He also drove on his ribbon of highway, stringing up and down the rolling hills and stretching plains and backwood hollers and the ancient farmland of the middle half of This Great Country (That's the way he'd always heard it pronounced where he'd grown up. *This Great Country.*)

The countryside he'd passed through was some of the richest farmland in the world. He passed mile after mile through the Piney Woods, through the Ozarks, through West Virginia coal mining country, into Pennsylvania. He drove into that state's coal country and then dropped southwards along the state's border, and into what is perhaps the best farmland of all.

But before that—along the way—along the seemingly interminable stretch of highway that is Tennessee, he'd stopped at one of his checkpoints.

"I knew yer daddy. He was a good man."

That was all the man had said to him. Then the man leaned into the window and shook Calvin's hand. He told Calvin that now he ought to have enough gas to get him to his next stopover.

"Tell Mr. Wall, when you see him, that Lem said hello."

Calvin nodded solemnly, and the old man put his foot on the kickboard and made a motion with his arms like he was slinging the truck outward into space, throwing his arms out, as if to say '*on your way!*'

Calvin pulled out along the winding road and out to the county highway, and the adventure continued.

He thought about home as he drove along. He thought about that word. *Home.* He thought about Texas. Then he thought about his dad. His dad had always had a kind of fluid identity. Maybe his dad had passed that on to him. Most men are, he thought, fluid beings. They either bend with the times, or they are of the sort that shape them. His mind had wandered, and he wondered whether he was a "*home is where you hang your hat*" kind of guy. Then he thought about the man who'd sent him on this journey, Mr. Wall. Jonathan Wall was a man who shaped the times. His name described him more than anything else did.

The rolling hills and the beautiful trees and the quiet of the nighttime sky whizzed by, and they all could have been waves on the ocean for all Calvin noticed them. He was riding on a train of thought down a track.

He tried to remember that one Whitman poem that talked about the guy walking under the stars... *That one chemist guy quoted it*, he thought. *The one from Breaking Bad. That one poem about the guy walking out and looking up at the nighttime stars, when Mr. White first started thinking that the other chemist might replace Jesse...* Calvin thought through the details of the show, seeing if he could get clues to remind him of the poem. He couldn't. He found himself wishing he had more cultural references that weren't derived from TV. He looked out over the darkness spread before him. Calvin was lost in thought as the miles rolled past.

He tried to remember that poem again but he couldn't remember it. He didn't really know it that well.

\*\*\*\*

He watched the road ahead of him the way a person who is getting sleepy watches the road. In a daze. That is perfectly understandable. It is in the nature of things.

Because it was midnight, and Calvin *was*, in fact, getting sleepy.

# Chapter 14
# Rescue

The lamps from Calvin's old Ford pickup threw a distinct pair of spotlights onto the roadway. They were not centered in the middle, aiming at some unified middle distance. They simply pointed straight forward out onto the roadway just in front of him...but only *just...* in front. Headlights are one of the things that did, indeed, improve over time.

The Ford's lights only revealed the world in stages. They lit up each successive field of vision only a slight... bit... further... ahead. Having driven mostly by instinct for an hour, flying mostly blind, Calvin was blurrily staring out into the dark of the middle distance. He was looking into the space that the lamps lit least. They shone out as if they were spotlights on a stage. They pointed downward from the balcony onto the stage of his life, which, right now, was the roadway. Seated in that balcony, he was only a spectator.

In the two globules of light, spread out and amplified by the white of the snow, framing the shot, were two yellow suits fighting for their lives.

They were fighting as if they wanted *to live*.

\* \* \* \*

Calvin saw them but he did not know, at first, what to make of them. It was a surreal vision. They were off in the further distance. The scene, gathering light, only came slowly into view. There were two groups of men. Boys, really. Fighting with the suits, trying to get them into several trailers or wagons parked along the road. The yellow suits were struggling to escape from their captors. The taller of the suits was reaching backwards, toward something lying in the road.

\* \* \* \*

Calvin can almost make it out. He can almost *see* what the thing is laying in the road. It is coming into his headlights. And then he is upon it. The miles and the yards and the feet... and the... *inches*... they all flew by him. He came to a dead forward thrusting standstill.

He heard the gas cans slosh behind him as the pickup rattled to a shuddering halt. *Sheesh!* He ducked his head down and held his breath, cringing. He'd heard of static electricity building up in gas cans that are not grounded blowing up like a bomb. He sniffed the air for any smell of leaked gas as he got out of the car and ran around to the front. He smelled no leaks and bent down to inspect the items in the road. Two bikes, with some bags strapped to them. Stepping out, he gathered both bikes and threw them into the back of his truck bed, moving deftly and staying low around the truck. He didn't know exactly why he was doing it, but it felt right, and he didn't argue with himself. He worked quickly and instinctively, without a plan other than to *help*. He swung around the door and jumped into the cab and realized that he had not turned off his lights on approach.

\* \* \* \*

Some of the men who'd been fighting with the yellow suits, the ones in motley military uniforms, were now coming towards him. They were shouting at him and waving their arms. Calvin could not make out what they were shouting but he did not need to.

He inched the vehicle forward, as if he were pulling up to ask directions. As if he were just some guy out on a Sunday drive and he'd taken a wrong turn. He came upon the first of the men who were walking back toward him. And he punched the truck forward. He pushed at the horn but with no effect. He was just ad-libbing now, an actor on the stage who didn't know his lines. He just did what felt right.

He swerved this way and that as the guards tried to run along beside him and reach into the cab. He swerved into the snow embankments on the sides of the road, spinning the wheel and the truck to shake the men off, and he just kept driving. The men in the uniforms up ahead, the ones fighting with the yellow suits, stopped and gawked at the spectacle. Everyone simply stopped for a moment as Calvin broke free and drove like a maniac toward the suits and toward the uniforms.

\* \* \* \*

There was a moment when, in the headlights of the pickup, Calvin saw in the eyes of the guards that they thought they might intimidate him. They raised their guns and pointed them directly at his head. They stood in the roadway as if they thought that would stop him. They thought that it would stop *anyone*. They can't be blamed much. It is in the nature of things. The guards were simply not accustomed to dealing with people who did not understand the underlying force implied in such situations. They lived, unconsciously, by the Maoist doctrine that truth was found in the barrel of a gun, and they were not accustomed to coming across people who were not familiar with such a truth. The guards weren't normally challenged in such a manner. But it didn't take them long to figure out that they didn't like it.

They stood in the roadway with their guns pointed at Calvin's head, and they wondered whether the driver of the approaching pickup knew just *who they were*. Did he know exactly *who he was dealing with*?

The answer to that question, had they bothered to actually ask it, would have been "Yes."

But that wasn't the problem.

The problem was not that Calvin did not know who the men in the road were, or that he did not see their guns, or that he did not assess the danger. Rather, it was exactly the opposite. The problem was that the soldiers in the road, pointing at him with their guns, thinking that threats were all that needed to be said on the matter, did not know Calvin Rhodes.

\* \* \* \*

The light of the headlamps bore down upon the guards and they scattered like cockroaches before it. One of the rear guards held his ground though. As the guard sighted down his gun to shoot though the windshield, Calvin leaned slightly to his left, and then turned his head towards the side glass. He prayed.

* * * *

As the bullet ripped through the windshield and the cab and then the back glass, missing Calvin's head by inches, he slammed on the brakes and the truck slipped sideways and struck the gunman with the passenger-side rear fender back by the bed. Calvin thought... *that guy ain't gonna make it...* and then he accelerated again, streaming by the other bandits, heading towards the yellow suits.

Calvin came upon the yellow suits as if in slow motion, and they looked like aliens, these people, in their hoods and breathing apparatus. They leaned toward his pickup, in the ball of light created by the ancient headlamps, and held up hands as if in supplication. Their bright yellow suits were set in contrast with the red of the truck, the green of the tarp, the white of the snow.

Calvin leaned over to look into the framing of his pickup truck's window. The taller suit leaned in to stare at him as he passed. *A face in a window.* The truck paused.

Time itself paused. It was a woman's face, looking out the plastic window of the hazmat helmet. Her breath momentarily, just for a micro-second, fogged up the shield of her helmet as he passed by, but then it cleared. Her startled visage was luminous in the nighttime glow. Not even for a moment did she look frightened. But she looked at Calvin, and he noticed it. And she mouthed the words *Help Us.*

* * *

*Get In!* He mouthed the words back at her. He pointed to the back of the pickup. The two yellow suits put their weight on the running boards and pushed their way up onto the bed, even as Calvin peeled out along the highway. He punched the gas and shifted gears, and they were almost fifty yards away before the bullets began to rain down on them. The shots, thankfully, were not very accurate. He was half a mile away before the sounds of gunfire faded into the night and were masked by the crunching of the tires on the road and the cold wind knifing through the bullet hole in the windscreen.

He'd learned from his recent mistakes, and, after the two yellow suits had piled into the bed of the truck, he'd flipped the headlights off. It's hard to hit what you cannot see, his father had told him. But now he was driving blindly through the night, and he tried his best to use the glow of the stars in the nighttime sky to drive by, watching intently for the faint reflection from the road that disappeared near its edges.

Kerthump.

Calvin heard it, but it didn't really register. Then it came again and again.

Kerthumkerthumpkerthump... kerthump!

He struggled to hold the wheel on the road, and as he gripped the wheel in a white-knuckled embrace, he became aware of the knocking on the window behind his head. The car rumbled and shook. The drive shaft shook too as he fought to keep control. He glanced at the gauges. He'd been doing sixty-something in the dark. Maybe more. Adrenaline exploded through his mind and body. The truck slowed to almost nothing, and the sound of muffled screams through the busted window behind his head. It was timed with the pounding of a fist on the cab top.

* * * *

Calvin had driven into a ditch. He was riding on four flats tires. *Blowouts,* he thought, *On all four, and all at once!*

He'd been blessed that the truck hadn't overturned... blessed to be alive.

He sniffed the air and jumped out of the cab. Again, no fumes. Calvin gave a little hop to look over the truck bed, where he saw a tangle of tarp and bikes and cans... and yellow hazmat suits. He looked in at the wriggling bodies inside the suits. The tallest of the them eventually righted itself and reached up to unbuckle its hood. It was the woman. The face in the window. The shorter suit was a boy, obviously her son. The resemblance was clear. They were beautiful, the two of them. Calvin smiled.

"Sorry about the ride."

"What?! Are you trying to kill us der, boy?"

Calvin looked at the woman, and then she smiled at him. It was all the thanks he needed, her smile. There was something poetic in it, the same quality that made people stand in front of the Mona Lisa and stare.

\* \* \* \*

Time flows on like a thread, weaving its stories together in odd and wonderful ways. Stephen has just been saved from a tragedy. He and his mother had almost been captured. If not for intervention, they would have been led to an almost certain... What *was* it, exactly?

He'd been riding along with his mother and then they'd been set upon by these bad guys and then there was this truck that came rattling out of nowhere and then they'd jumped into the back of the truck.

Then they'd fled wildly through darkness in the back of the truck. That part had been amazing... and frightening. Still, there'd been this moment of overwhelming freedom... of *salvation.*

And then there was the crash.

* * * *

Stephen sat up, at last. After struggling through the tarp and rolling around on the cans and having the bicycles poking him in the ribs, he'd finally been able to right himself, and had taken off his helmet. He saw his mother already looking at the guy who'd just saved them. He was short and Chinese. Stephen's own age... maybe a few years older. Still a teenager though. He looked at his mother and he looked at the guy and he thought how it seemed that they'd already exchanged words. They just seemed to have that connection, as if they were past making introductions.

He focused in on the words they did say.

"Sorry about the ride."

"What?! Are you trying to kill us der, boy?"

Stephen looked at his mother. He'd noticed that her accent was coming out with the stress of the travel. He looked at the guy who had just saved them, and they both broke into a grin. Stephen jabbed his mom in the ribs. "Kill us *der...* mom? *Der?* Really?"

Stephen smiled at Calvin again and nodded his head to the older youth. He did it in a way that said *Hey, nice rescue and stuff.* Calvin looked at the two of them, these yellow suits, whom he'd just rescued from a gunfight in a snowfield... and he screwed up his face. It should have been an awkward moment, but it wasn't.

He looked at them with his most inquisitive look... and asked, "Hey... got anything to eat?"

* * * *

"You looked like those guys on Breaking Bad," Calvin said. There he was again, referring to a television show. The two of them just laughed.

"Yeah, I guess we did," Stephen answered. "Good thing, too. I was about to go all Heisenberg on them." Calvin and Stephen laughed again. They were sitting with their backs against the truck while Veronica scouted out an area to see if she could find some little nook or cranny where they might hide throughout the night.

"We'll attend to the vehicle in the morning," she said. And then she'd gone to scout.

She'd only been gone fifteen minutes, and the two teens were already talking like old friends, remembering what that *other* world was like, as if it weren't really gone.

"Dude... did you see that one show that was going to come out on F/X?" Stephen paused. That was one way to tell that the boys were beginning to reckon with the new world. They'd begun to talk about the old life in tenses that showed they'd once thought for a moment that it might return, but now they no longer did.

"Yeah ... that show that was gonna be about Russian spies in America? What was it gonna to be called?"

"Oh yeahyeahyeah. That one from the Cold War, with Reagan and Michael Jackson and stuff. Ummm, *The Americans*?" Stephen said, nodding his head. "I saw the preview. It looked like it was going to be good."

"Dude, that chick on that show was hot," Calvin said, looking at Stephen and smiling. "She looked like she could kick some butt."

"Yeah," Stephen said. He smiled and thought of a girl in a bodega in that other world. "I'd betray my country for a chick like that."

"Yeah... a chick like that, or..." Calvin made a little mock motion of sniffing the air, "some French fries."

Veronica could hear their guffaws from several hundred yards away as she walked toward them in silence through the night.

\* \* \* \*

Veronica stayed up through the night, watching. She had her pistol and she hoped she'd never be forced to use it. They'd walked a good quarter-mile into the forest before bedding down for the night. Stephen and Calvin slept in fits and starts. Before morning broke, she roused them, and they put on their clothes while she put out some food for them. She hummed a song under her breath, and occasionally she'd break out into a small bit of lyric. She sang the line in its lilting sing-song herkyjerkyness. She swung her head to the side when she did it, her long ropy braids whipping over her shoulder. Then she stopped, and caught herself. She'd thought she was humming under her breath, but she'd actually sung out loud. She stopped, and the boys looked at her. She was caught like a deer in the headlights.

"What's that song, Mrs. D?" Calvin was already fitting in the way that kids like Calvin do... seamlessly. He was already calling her "Mrs. D." He looked at her, expectantly.

"Oh, just a song that I was listening to before..." Veronica said. As she did so, she waved out into the nothingness, as if to say *all this*. Stephen rolled his eyes. "Oh, again, with the Clay stuff." Veronica cut him a sharp glance. It was clear that whatever "the Clay stuff" was had been a topic of some conversation between them. Calvin looked at them both, wondering what he'd stepped into.

"There was this guy that came by our house during the storm." Stephen indicated with his hand somewhere *back there.* "He was cool. He and my mom connected. They listened to this group called the Mountain Goats, and..." He rolled his eyes at his mom.

"What? It's a good song," Veronica said.

"I agree," Calvin said. Stephen looked at him sideways like a sibling who realizes he has competition. Stephen made a mock look of pain.

"No, really. They're cool," Calvin said. "I mean, I haven't heard the *new* new stuff, but they are always good." He let that hang in the air. Stephen stepped back as if to say *You're killing me.*

Veronica laughed at their antics. "The thing that *really* bothers Stephen about the Clay *situation...*" Veronica said, nodding her head to Stephen as if they'd had this conversation before... "I may have overstepped my bounds when the man stayed with us. I took some poems of his and had them bound without his permission. Stephen thought that what I did was a horrible breach of privacy. But I couldn't help myself." She looked at Stephen and he looked at Calvin. "Well, some of them were..." she searched through the air to find the word, "lovely."

They were walking low along a hedge at the edge of a paddock, keeping their eyes peeled across the pristine field of white. The boys could tell that she was bound to go on and so they let her. "There was this one poem that described a

Van Gogh painting. And I *love* Van Gogh. It was partly him who led me to paint! Anyway, the poem described the lush fields and broken doors on their hinges, and the sea, and the sea of faces that are found in his paintings. But it was more than just about the color. It was also about the loneliness of being Van Gogh, in his brilliance, and his madness. We almost never knew him, you know? It was only through the support and the promotion of his brother that he became well-known. Otherwise, he was an outcast. In Gauguin, he had a friend who seemed to understand him, but Gauguin was always *promising* to come and see him. He rarely did..."

Veronica and the boys walked circumspectly as they talked. She indicated to the wider world with her hand, the white of the field, the hint of blue invading the gray of the morning sky. "Anyway," she said, "it was a lovely poem."

And with that, Calvin, Stephen, and Veronica found themselves standing at the back bumper of the rusted red pickup truck in the brown-white slush of the accident. "It was a nail strip," Veronica told them. "I found it last night when I was out on patrol. Whoever put it there will be around soon enough to check it. We have to work quickly."

Standing in the thin blue light of morning, their breath rose up before them. It rose in little puffs against the coldness of the air.

From the Poems of C.L. Richter

*A question*

*And what is to stop a Van Gogh –*
*Weary from too many Arlesienne nights lost in a haze of whores and absinthe,*
*Mad from waiting for a Gauguin, who never comes, to come –*

*From getting up from his makeshift bed, loose-joined planks creaking under the weight of his rising shift, tangled sheets clamoring, twisting underneath him, stretching out their gnarled arms to hold down his gaunt form,*
*From dressing in his threadbare clothes, simple sepia-toned, basket-woven fabrics, dried on a hook, stiffened, still-containing smells of flesh, earth and sea-breeze,*
*From running his thin, rangy hands across his haggard face, five days growth of shocking redorange beard skeining through his fingertips, rioting against the calm in the browns of his shirt, the blues of the walls, his own fleshy tones,*
*From binding up his canvases, hands stippled with spikes of pure color, soft as leather, strong like wire, and lacing the binding under his arm, his ragged hat cocked slightly on his head, pulled over one ear, shading light over one eye,*
*From walking out of his cottage, down the pebbled pathway, redbrown door swinging slightly ajar, quivering uncertainly in the thin morning light,*
*From walking along a broken trail and, at its end, across a golden field,*

*autumn grass bending in a breezy sway, nodding toward a still further field where sunflowers rise like soldiers, their sharp sentry eyes scanning the surrounding hills, warily watching a row of greenbrown olive trees congregating at the edge of the plowline, their smaller hedges rising up like smoke in wispy branches,*

*From traversing the field in sharp diagonal lines that lengthen out and flatten as the hills give way to coastline and miles of organic biomass teeming in a salty, towing surf, heard before it can be seen, smelled before it can be heard,*

*From finding a small yellowblue dinghy tied along the greengrey waterline and fashioning a makeshift sail out of stitched-together canvases, hoisted up the boom and creaking against the rigging as they unfurl and expand to reveal radiant flowers, swirling firmament, and boldly textured faces in the shimmering sunlight,*

*And from loosening the mooring, leaning his weight into the pull of the halyards, and setting off towards the distant horizon, where line and form are one?*

# Chapter 15
# War

The shot and the echo of the shot rang out across the little clearing and bounced up into the trees and then the sky.

Peter turned and saw the man on horseback, his arm raised, holding a rifle at a right angle to his body. His brain at first refused to believe the information being transported to it by his sleepy eyes. A puff of smoke trailed across the clearing and lifted up to the heavens. A warning shot. The man brought down the rifle and aimed straight at Peter. He wouldn't warn again. His uniform was that of the Missouri National Guard.

Peter understood enough of what was occurring to know that he should not raise his own rifle. He put his hands in the air, and from around him appeared other soldiers who swooped down on him like hawks. They disarmed him and pulled his hands behind his back.

The man on the horse, the one with the rifle, was lecturing him about the new laws. Specifically, the man was telling him that it was a death penalty offense to be carrying a weapon of any kind. The officer droned on for a moment, the horse turning from side to side, as Peter was led to a tree at the edge of the clearing. It took the entirety of this time for Peter to become cogent enough to understand that he was not in a dream.

The man ordered the other soldiers to tie Peter to the tree, and they did so without any hesitation. It was at this point when reality zoomed back into focus, the brain sleep cleared, the adrenaline began pumping, and Peter realized that he was seconds away from being shot.

\* \* \* \*

When the firing started from down the hill, the man on horseback, the leader of this Missouri National Guard unit, was sighting down his rifle and just about to pull the trigger in order to execute Peter for the crime of having a gun. Shots rang out from down the hill, and instead of pulling the trigger, he looked down just in time to see the second soldier, who was attempting ingress into the cabin, fall mortally wounded.

During that millisecond when his eyes cut to the cabin, his rifle swayed. It was a tiny motion. Perhaps involuntary, but it was enough. He had to take just a tiny second longer to steady his aim, sitting on the horse. And at that moment, almost the instant he found his target again, his head burst into a spray of blood, brains, and bone.

The body toppled off the horse, and as the dead officer's blood began to pump into the snowy ground, his body writhed. Two more of his men dropped in succession—felled by bullets fired from somewhere in the distance... from some unknown source.

The shots that killed the soldiers could only be faintly identified as sharp cracks piercing the crisp morning air. The sound echoed for a moment and then was gone. The remaining soldiers began to drop to the ground in panic, and they attempted to crawl back over the low rise, but before they could find cover, two more of them were shot dead from afar. It was a turkey shoot.

\* \* \* \*

Lang awoke to the sound of gunfire. Really close gunfire. He remembered waking up this way that last morning in Warwick, and he instinctively rolled over and felt the pain shoot up his wounded arm. It was a different pain, and his brain registered the difference. He was feeling better, he could tell. The sugar cure was working, and even without any food last night or breakfast this morning, he felt like life was returning into him. He'd gone to sleep not knowing if he would ever wake up again, but now he was awake, and the gunfire gave impetus to his feelings of being free and alive. However, now there was shooting going on, and he needed to find out what it was all about.

He low-crawled into the hallway and saw a dead soldier slumped over the broken wood of the door, and could see another dead soldier only a few feet outside the entryway, splayed backwards and bleeding from his mouth and nose.

Lang heard shuffling and felt a strong tug on the back of his jacket. He looked up to see Natasha and Elsie pulling him. He lurched to help them, and they dragged him out from the sightlines of the doorway and into the front bedroom. He looked around at the room. It was the one that Natasha had first rolled into when the men tried to invade the cabin. He rolled up on his shoulder and, just as he did, more gunfire shattered the morning. Bullets pierced through the walls like they didn't even exist, Lang noticed, as little holes of light appeared in the walls and streams of sunshine flowed through the little holes and splashed across the floor in tight lines. *A wooden building is not a great place to be in a battle,* he thought.

"Nope. Not this room!" Natasha shouted, and now Lang was being dragged again, like a mannequin, past the hallway and into the kitchen. Natasha had noticed when they'd first entered the cabin that the exterior walls of the kitchen had been made of heavy field stone. If she remembered correctly, the stone went at least four feet up the surface. Natasha, Elsie, and Lang stumbled in their low crawls into the kitchen area as the cabin began to rock with the gunfire that relentlessly pierced the structure.

\* \* \* \*

Kent was sick. He could feel his stomach spasm, and the stew and vodka tumbled around in his gut and would not settle. It was not the food and drink from the previous night that had made Kent sick... at least it was not *primarily* the food and drink. He was sick of everything. Mostly he was sick of Val.

"Damn, are you drunk, again, pudgy boy?"

It was Val, talking over his shoulder. Val had become for the round-faced young man a symbol of everything that made him sick... of everything that was making the world sick.

"I drank but one cup last night," Kent muttered under his breath. The alcohol sloshed in his stomach. He knew that probably wasn't true.

\* \* \* \*

The four were struggling up a sharp incline, and Mike had ordered Kent to carry the new backpack—the one they'd just taken from the man that Val had killed.

The four travelers had stumbled upon the man sobbing in the woods. He was wearing what might have once been a business suit, and he didn't hear the approaching party until it was too late. In fright, he'd spun around, and as he did so, he lifted a hunting knife, and before he could even rightly wield it or threaten anyone with the instrument, Val had kicked it clean out of the man's hand.

What had happened next was the reason that Kent was sick.

The man had immediately dropped to the ground and had begun pleading for his life. His story spilled from him like water over a dam. The story went by so fast that it was hard to make out, but Kent had gotten the gist of it.

The man and two of his friends had been traveling on behalf of the Governor of Pennsylvania when all the cars had stopped on the highway (the EMP, Kent noted.) The three men tried to escape the horrors of the highway by making their way through the woods, but, in the last few days, both of his friends had been killed.

While the man whimpered and sobbed through his story, Val was busy rifling through the man's backpack and noticed that it was full of survival gear, ammunition, and food and even an ammo can with a radio and other electrical devices.

"Where'd you get all the swell survival gear... huh?" Val asked with an accusation in his voice. "I'm pretty sure that Governor's aids don't carry this kind of gear on business trips."

"Uhh... ahhh... well, we just came upon it," the man answered. Guilt and shame were evident on the man's face, and this, more than anything, enraged the brutish Val.

Val stopped his rummaging and walked over to the man and kicked him straight in the face as hard as he possibly could. Kent noted to himself that it was remarkable what a boot can do to a human face. Remarkable and grotesque. The man, bloody face buried in the snow, began sobbing again, and now he'd locked down completely. Emotionally and mentally the man was just spent. He didn't respond to any of Val's questions, and this struck Val as a lack of the proper respect he thought he was due. Mike, Steve, and Kent had all tried to stop him, but Val began to stomp the man, and in short order, he'd succeeded in leaving behind a bloody corpse.

This is why Kent was sick to his stomach.

\* \* \* \*

Elsie's mind was churning, and her eyes flicked from left to right as she tried to calculate and understand everything that was happening.

She shouted it. "Peter!"

"He's up on the ridge!" Lang said over the thwacks and zings of bullets coming through the building.

"I've got to get to him," Elsie whispered.

"You can't go out there, Elsie," Natasha said. "They'll cut you down."

"I can go out the back. The firing is starting to slow down, and it has all come from the front. I'll run out and keep low and get into the trees and then work my way up to the ridge."

She looked at them. "I have to." She had the beginnings of a tear in her eye. "He's up there all alone."

"Peter can take care of himself," Lang said, a little too sharply.

"He's not up there taking care of himself, young man." Elsie shot back. "He's up there taking care of *us*."

"If you go," Natasha said, as debris from the walls rained down around them, "take Lang's backpack... in case you get lost, or we don't make it."

"You'll make it, Natasha. Both of you will. I just know it!"

Natasha smiled amid the horrors. *Nothing like a Pollyanna to give you hope when the world is collapsing on your head.*

Elsie saw Natasha's smile and returned it. Then she broke for the back door, picking up Lang's pack and throwing it over her shoulder on her way out.

Lang grabbed the .22 and Natasha lifted the pistol. Both weapons were woefully inappropriate for such a gunfight. Still, both of them began to tug at the carpets that covered the windows so that they could lay down some covering fire for Elsie. They did this because both Natasha and Lang were thinking about Elsie and Peter and not about themselves.

\* \* \* \*

Kent had finally made it up to the top of the grade when he felt his gorge rise, and in a second he was doubled over, vomiting onto the snow and rocks.

"Great," Val sneered. "What a winner you turned out to be. Just look at you. I'm sick of your weakness!"

Kent wiped his mouth with his sleeve and dropped the pack. He took a step towards Val, "Then why don't you try to stomp me to death you sadistic bastard!"

Val seemed willing to do just that, but Steve and Mike jumped between the two before any more violence could commence. After the two men had been pulled apart, Mike stepped into Val's space and put his face only inches from the brutish man's nose. Val was a full foot taller, but Mike's presence had a weight and gravity all of its own.

"One more argument," Mike said. He cleared his throat. "One more threat. One more unauthorized stomping. One more unauthorized *anything* from you Vladimir, and I'll kill you myself. Do you understand me, Comrade?"

The man who now called himself Val dropped his eyes and took a step back. "I understand, Comrade Mikail Mikailivitch."

Mike looked over to Kent and pointed to the fallen backpack.

"Pick it up."

Kent did.

He didn't even think to ask why.

\* \* \* \*

The four men fell back into line, and as they hiked in a southwesterly direction, they saw the valley open up below them, and Kent was glad that, at least for a little while, they'd be walking downhill.

He took up the rear, right behind Val, and as the group marched forward through the snow, Kent whispered so that just Val could hear him.

"I called you a sadistic bastard because you are literally a sadist and the fatherless son of a whore. So there's that, Vladimir. And, also this... before this is over, I am going to kill you."

Death and violence have a tendency to multiply when the shackles of civility are thrown off. Men who are violent and rapacious killers can be identified more readily, and men who might otherwise be peaceful and passive are sometimes not able to resist the desire to rid the world of soulless predators. There are such men even among the poets.

\* \* \* \*

Elsie sprinted towards the trees and bullets zipped around her. Snow popped up into the air where the shots plowed into the ground. She could hear that gunfire was being returned from the cabin, and she could see the pops popping at her feet. Then the shots that were loosely aimed in her direction stopped, but she did not.

Rounding the edge of the hill, she was surprised to meet up with Peter who was on his way down toward the rear of the cabin. He had the AK-47 at the ready, and he grabbed Elsie by the arm and pulled her over to a stand of trees, and they crawled into the brush near the base of the stand.

"How'd you get out of there?" Peter asked.

"Natasha and Lang covered me," Elsie answered, breathlessly.

"Why didn't they escape with you?"

"Lang is better, but he is in no condition to travel. Natasha would never leave him. I would have stayed too, but I thought... I ought to find out what happened to you. We..." she indicated to the cabin with her hand. She tried to brush a wisp of hair away. She tried to do it with the gentleness of her fingertips, but they were clammy with dried blood, so instead she raised the sweaty backside of her arm to her forehead and wiped away the strand. "We... we thought you might be dead," Elsie said, her eyes dropped to look at her knees in the snow.

"I'm not dead... but I almost was. I was captured on the ridge up there by the Missouri Guard. They were going to execute me."

Elsie sucked in her breath. "I'm sorry." Peter shook it off as if to say *no need*. "How'd you get off that ridge, Peter?" Elsie asked.

Peter looked at her and shrugged. The knowledge that he would certainly have been dead by now was fully upon him as he stared at Elsie. He smiled a crooked smile and said one word...

"Ace."

\* \* \* \*

The sounds of gunfire from the battle grew louder as Mike, Steve, Val, and Kent moved to the southwest. They came to a ridge, approaching from the northeast, and they crawled up to the top of it to see if they could make out what the fuss was all about.

What they saw shocked them. At the top of the ridge were a number of dead bodies. All the corpses were in uniform, and Mike, crawling to one of the men who had been shot in the back of the head and saw the insignia for the Missouri National Guard on the uniform.

Looking down from the ridge, they saw that a gunfight had erupted around a small cabin. Forces in the woods opposite the front door of the cabin were pouring fire into the structure, while every once in a while random and impotent shots would ring out, fired from the windows of the cabin itself.

Staying as low as possible, Mike, Steve, and Val moved quickly, checking the bodies of the dead soldiers for weapons, ammunition, or other valuables. Kent, meanwhile, had come across another body—this one looked to be the corpse of an officer—and he discreetly secured a pistol he found on the ground near the body.

Mike never saw Kent take the gun. He was now busy spying out the battle taking place below him. He heard a sharp crack from the distance ring out. He could not make out from where the shot was coming, but he saw one of the soldiers from among the contingent assailing the cabin fall dead.

Another crack from the distance, and another soldier fell. Mike's eyes began to scan the hills in the distance to the east. He knew from his training what was happening...

Sniper.

# Chapter 16
# Team Clay

Veronica said, "Okay, now this is what we're going to do, boys." They looked at her expectantly. "My dad was a resourceful guy. Back when he was doing work on the faraway settlements in Trinidad, he saw these Indian guys packing straw into their tires, because there was no compressed air to be had."

"Yes!" Calvin said, excitedly. Veronica and Stephen looked at him with startled looks on their faces. It was something in the way he said that *Yes...* He made it sound like he had more important things to say on the manner. So they let him speak.

"My dad... He was a pharmaceutical engineer... in China. Back before the crackdown. During it, really..." He paused and looked at them.

It should have been strange. Just last night he'd rescued these two strangers from a gun battle, and now he was telling them

175

things... *things about his dad.* It should have been strange. But it wasn't.

He continued. "Yeah, so my dad, he told me this story about how the Chinese government sent him to the outback... you know, down in Australia. They wanted him to find this one plant or something, to make an assessment of its chemical potential on the spot." He paused. "They were testing him." Calvin felt a little flush rise in his cheeks, just a hint of anger. He looked at the two of them, and then remembered where he was, and what he was doing. He blushed in full.

"But anyway, he told me some natives did just that. They simply rolled the car over on its top and filled all four tires with straw, all at once. My dad said those guys were like a Daytona pit crew, just all wild and crazy. Detailed *and* quick *and* efficient. They packed the grass and straw together, wetting it down. If they had water handy, they'd mix it with thick mud, like cob. They'd bend it into the curves of the tire and then pound it in with rocks." He rubbed his face with his hand. "If they didn't have water, they just packed the grass and straw really tight... just pound it as tight as they could get it with the stones.

Veronica and Stephen smiled at the image.

"Strong at the broken places..." Veronica whispered, under her breath.

"Ma'am?" Calvin stuttered.

"Oh, 'strong at the broken places.' It's something Hemingway wrote. I was thinking how the straw in a way becomes strong... inside the tire, by bending, by bonding with the others. By utilizing both its tensile and flexile strength..."

Her voice trailed off at the end of the sentence. She'd seen the hurt in Calvin's eyes when he talked about his father.

She'd also heard the anger in his voice, although she did not know where that anger came from. Veronica knew, without his having to say it, that Calvin had lost his father. She wanted to say something to help him, but she realized that, in this time, there was not much room for such niceties. Still, she wanted to him know. She wanted to say the words... *We know. We've lost someone, too...*

\* \* \* \*

"And I was also thinking of you, young man!"

Veronica turned to Calvin, who looked startled. "You've lost your father. Anyone who has eyes to see can see that. My son has lost his father, too." She paused, and looked at Stephen. "And I have lost a husband. But... we become strong at the broken places. Even here." She placed her hand to her heart, her hand in a fist. She tapped her heart two times. Calvin looked at her, and he wanted to say something, *anything*, to let her know that he understood.

"And here you are, young man. You have been given to us a second time. First, with the truck and now... well, with the truck again." She indicated with her hand to the tires. "You know how to do this good work, because your father passed that knowledge down to you." She looked at him as if to say that Stephen would be his brother now. As if they would look out for each other... and she would play mother hen... "So. Do you see?"

She pointed to the tires, ground down to the nubbins. She pointed to a toolbox and a jack that she'd pulled out for them. She pointed to the ruts in the ground and the tires buried in them. "Strong in the broken places." She clapped her hands together. "Let's go. Let's get this done!" The boys grinned. They were laughing to see her happy. She had the kind of smile that made a person happy just to see it.

177

"Calvin, you organize. Stephen, help him and keep him honest. Do one tire at a time, and do it right the first time. Do you hear me? The first time! Lay it in thick. And tight. Pound it in with a rock... I am going to walk out on the road and keep a watch out. If you hear a shot, any kind of gun fire... Hide in the forest and wait for me. Do you hear me?" The boys nodded. And with that, she was gone.

\* \* \* \*

Calvin unfastened the green tarp, then pulled it down from the bed of the truck. He laid it out on top of a small, raised area of grass that stuck up above the snow. The truck, sliding off of the roadway, had dug deep and muddy ruts into the snow, and now the brown ruts were stark against the frozen white. He and Stephen shoveled wet mud onto the tarp until they had a good coating covering the center of the green, maybe three inches thick. Then they walked over to the fence line and anywhere else where the grass grew up through the snow, and they gathered armloads of organic material... grass, straw, weeds, and hay... anything.

Then they did the mud dance.

They stomped on the mixture for five to ten minutes at a time, then Calvin would pull one end of the tarp and then the other to flip over the "dough" that they were making, then they'd stomp it again. As they stomped, they talked and laughed like brothers. They made up a rap called the mud rap, and each one added a verse each time as they stomped heartily in the cold morning.

When the straw and mud were thoroughly mixed, they dumped the whole pile near one of the rear tires of the truck, and then began the whole process again.

This process went on for over an hour, and at the end of that time, they had enough mud/cob mixture to fill the tires.

Next, they jacked up the truck and removed the tires one at a time. Calvin showed them how to use the tire iron as a lever to remove the rubber from the bead without pulling off the whole tire. Then they stuffed. They stuffed and stuffed. And they pounded. Pounded and pounded.

When they could not get another ounce of cob into the tires, they finished, remounted the tire, and went to the next one.

"When we drive down the road, the cob will heat up and expand and fill what's left of the cavity," Calvin said.

"Are you sure?" Stephen asked.

"No!"

"You aren't sure?"

"Nope! I've never done this before! I just told you that my father saw it done. It's supposed to work, though."

\* \* \* \*

"Dude, your mom's kind of intense," said Calvin as they were pounding the cob down into the last tire with a rock that they'd found in the woods. The truck had slid down an embankment and down a smallish hill. They both knew it would take all the strength they could muster to get it up the hill, back onto the road, even under ideal conditions. They were working to better their odds.

"Yeah, she is." Stephen looked into the distance, as if he were thinking of another time.

"What happened to your dad?"

"Oh, he was killed in a subway accident. Years ago. He gave up his life saving this woman he didn't know. Jumped down on the tracks and lifted her up and..." He split his hands apart, helpless to find the words.

"Yeah, people called my dad a hero, too. He died to *keep* from hurting someone else." Stephen looked at him blankly. Calvin continued, "It's not really the same thing, but it is. Kind of."

"Yeah, bro. I hear you."

So, the conversation went on this way. The boys talked and worked. Occasionally, Veronica would come back to check on them, and she would encourage them through the process. She would always mix her little pep talks with object lessons. The boys would listen intently, and, as the sun crept across the morning sky and started to blend into afternoon, they completed their work.

\* \* \* \*

The line of military-style vehicles pulled up in a straight edge on a long road that ran through the heart of Pennsylvania farm country. The lead vehicle, an odd looking RV that seemed to have some kind of plated armor that made it, from a distance, look like a spaceship or a dinosaur, pulled into a small rounded driveway. Had one viewed the scene from the sky, the military convoy would have appeared to be pulled along the grids of roads by capillary action. The drivers were driving with purpose toward a destination known, apparently, only to themselves.

They pulled into the small driveway and stopped at a checkpoint in front of a gate. The men driving the military vehicles showed some kind of credentials, and then there was a conference, and they were let into the gate. The vehicles drove down the small driveway and dipped along a long winding road that led up to a farmhouse. They pulled in with practiced precision and lined up in beautifully stacked rows. The vehicles were orderly in their performance and worked together as one in a mechanical ballet.

The last few vehicles did not enter the driveway. They didn't stop at the checkpoint and they didn't follow the others up to the farmhouse. These few continued down the farm road, heading somewhere else.

* * * *

The RV was now parked behind the farmhouse. Inside the odd-shaped RV sat two men. One of the men looked like a cowboy, and the other looked like a leprechaun. A wee bit, anyway. They got out of the lead vehicle, the cowboy and the leprechaun, and they walked up to the doorway of the farmhouse. From a distance one could make out through the late afternoon haze the cowboy tipping his hat to the person who opened the door. The cowboy tipped his hat, and the leprechaun bowed at the waist. The leprechaun did a little dipsy-doodle shuffle of his feet as he walked in behind the cowboy, and the door was shut behind them.

* * * *

Red Beard looked at Clive. Red Beard's real name was Pat, but by now we all know him as Red Beard. That's what Clive called him, too. The two men found themselves seated in an old-fashioned drawing room. In the corner of the room was a small, simple table with a kerosene lamp. The light was evening out in fine shadows across the floor. Red Beard leaned back in his chair and said, "Let me tell you a story..."

Clive looked at Red Beard. "Tell it."

Red Beard looked at Clive again. "Well, I think I will...

"There was once this man who started a business. It was a small business. The man struggled. He scrimped and saved. He beat the bushes to find new customers and worked the ice cream socials at the local church. He joined the PTA." Red Beard paused. Clive put his hand out, as if to stop him.

"But did the tax man get his share? That's all I care to know." Clive flashed his best Sam Elliot smile. Red Beard spread his hands out before him.

"Of course. Indeed."

He continued. "So, his business was coming down to a crisis. It was one of those situations where sometimes you get the bear," he paused, "and sometimes the bear gets you... but, in this case, the bear was just about to have the final say."

Clive put his hand out to stop him again. "You know if you change *bear* to *beer* in that story, it still reads the same...?" He chuckled to himself and Red Beard paused.

Again, he smiled. "Indeed, it does."

"So, the man finally begins to make it," Red Beard said, "you know? And he hires a sales force. And his tippy-top sales guy... his very, *very* best... turns out to be a loafer."

Red Beard leaned over to whisper to Clive, as if conspiratorially, "I lean and loaf, at my ease..." He indicated with his hand across the ground... "observing a spear of summer grass..." He acted out the drama, and looked at Clive as if the words spoke for themselves. He wanted Clive to *know* that he had an eye for such things. He was a loafer, he seemed to say, but practiced and studious about it.

Clive also looked down at his feet... at their feet. He too imagined how lush and green this farmland was... the imaginary farmland under their feet... how valuable it could be.

\* \* \* \*

"So what happened to yer feller? The loafer?" Clive watched as Red Beard came back into his thoughts. Clive had never left his.

"So, this guy's sales force was incensed. Right? The whole lot of them. As a group. Pissed off. They couldn't put up with such debasement. Naturally, it did not matter to them that the loafer had the best numbers in the office. How did he get them?! *That* was the question. And the loafer didn't help his cause any. He'd spend a couple of hours a day doing his sales calls, and then he'd go across the street to the Y and play cards. He'd gamble all day with his feet on the table. On the table! Can you imagine it?

"So, you can imagine the consternation of the crowd. The business owner hired a consultant. He asked him to solve the problem. The consultant did a month long study of the problem, looking at the business, its productivity, it camaraderie, the social cohesion, morale, and the experience of the layout of the hermeneutical biodegradable whatever, whatever, the whatever... The consultant went through whole shebang, got it?

"And the consultant came to a final conclusion and put his answer in a one sentence report. *Get rid of the whole office and hire ten more like the loafer.*"

Red Beard indicated with his hand the lush bounty at their feet. He held up his ragged boots, as if he were looking past them into springtime, as if he and Clive were, at that moment, in a green field with cold beers in their hands, steaks on the grill, kids running through the sprinklers on the lawn. He looked down at his feet and saw them as if lightly resting on the long wispy strands of grass on the lawn of a warm spring afternoon in the ancient green of Pennsylvania.

\* \* \* \*

Clive indicated with his hand to the ground.

"May I?" he said, with a low sleep of his arm.

"Please do," Red Beard answered, and settled back in his chair for the ride.

"That's what we're doing here," Clive indicated with his thumb and forefinger to both the time and the place. "We're firing the lot of 'em... both the criminals who corrupted capitalism and turned it into a private candy store, and the democratic socialists who want to steal everything and then run the world. Believe it or not, the fascists are working with the communists. We're clearing the decks of the lot of 'em. We didn't start this war, but we saw it comin'. People won't get it because they can't see the whole thing yet. Maybe they think we're terrorists or something. They'll never understand the Luddites until a new world gets built on the old one. They still think the Russians and Americans are goin' at it, when in reality the powers that be... the banksters, the globalists, and the international socialists are the ones having a go at the people. They didn't expect us to muddle with their business, but we're doin' it anyway.

"We didn't set off the EMP. The commies did, and they did it with the help and aid of the corporatists and the globalists. The old-guard Soviets built the micro-nuke in North Korea while our folks twiddled their thumbs and guaranteed the people there wasn't a threat. Nope. We didn't start the fire, but we knew it was coming, and we let it happen because the world needed a re-start.

"But we're not gonna let 'em do what they have planned. The invasions will never happen. Their forces aren't going to regroup, because we'll hit them every time they get started. They can't see us, and we're everywhere. We're a Luddite army, and this time we've got the best toys. Just the irony alone is worth the expense."

Clive concluded his story, and, when he did, he looked over at Red Beard, and he saw that the man was riveted.

Red Beard smiled. "Do you think that maybe your plan is a bit hypocritical and... just a tad morally ambiguous?"

"Of course."

"Okay then."

"Twain said that *history doesn't repeat itself*, my friend," Clive began. Red Beard held up his hand as if to let Clive know that he would finish the sentence, this time, for him.

"*But it rhymes.*"

\* \* \* \*

Red Beard listened to Clive go on for a while longer. The glow from the kerosene heater in the corner of the room made his beard glow along with it. Its orange hue was set off by the umbered darkening air of the evening. The light began to fade. They both glowed as they sat in the chairs, waiting there in the drawing room. They shared more conversation and were electric with ideas. And ideals. They glowed in their seats.

They felt like... equals.

Neither of them cast a shadow.

* * * *

Veronica and the boys had pushed and pulled for a half hour, but to no avail. This light was beginning to fade, and she knew they could not be out here another night. "We *can* do this," Veronica encouraged them. "We just have to find the Archimedean point!" She gave a grunt as she said the last word, lifting up on a branch she had wedged under the bumper, trying to find a solid place in the sludge under the truck from which to gain leverage. The truck bumped a little. Calvin and Stephen heaved just as she did the lift again, and the truck bumped once more. "Okay, boys. I might have found the sweet spot. We just need to put more rocks under the wheel over there," she indicated with her hand toward the rear tire, "so we can get more traction..." Stephen placed some small rocks under the tire as she lifted on the branch. "And Calvin keep it in low, and give it a little gas ..." Veronica paused to make sure both boys were ready. She took a breath.

"And... Heave!"

* * * *

Sometimes in life, the narrative steps sideways. It simply takes a step to the left or the right. Whichever way you want to imagine it. Like when you close your left eye and you see a slightly different world than when you close you right eye. Time shifts, in inches. The world becomes different... but only slightly different.

\*\*\*\*

Veronica lifted with all her might. She leaned into the branch and lifted from her knees, from her loins, from her heart. Stephen stood at the back bumper with his mother. He shifted his feet in the sludge and tried to find solid footing from which to push. He leaned his shoulder into the bumper and gave it his all. Calvin jerked his body forward slightly in the bucket seat, as if that would help with the momentum, and gave the truck a little gas.

It caught, just slightly. The truck rocked back just a bit, and Veronica lifted again, getting her shoulder under the branch. Calvin heard the whine and felt the blessed pull of forward momentum. Stephen slipped in the sludge once the tires caught, and in Calvin's excitement at applying pressure to the gas pedal, the truck lurched forward and pulled up into the track from the night before.

The truck was on the roadway before Calvin saw the two military vehicles bearing down upon him with frightening speed. He was out of the truck before the men with guns had stopped their vehicles and spread out along the roadside. Stephen and Veronica came up out of the ditch and saw the men standing there and looked at Calvin and he looked at them. The soldiers raised their guns. Calvin stepped into the middle of the road and did a little hop, raising one hand in the air and reaching into his back pocket for something.

*A piece of paper.*

The guards rattled their guns, and Calvin came out of his little hop, caught himself and stood up taller and held both his hands high in the air. The white paper in one hand, now unfolded, spilled out of his fist like a flag of surrender. He offered it to the guards, and one of them made a little motion toward him, as if to accept it.

"It's OKAY. It's OKAY," Calvin said, with his hands still raised above his head. The men with the guns pointed at him, and then rattled, and then relaxed with Calvin's next words.

"I'm with Jonathan Wall."

The gun barrels dropped toward the ground in unison.

\* \* \* \*

The stream of life sometimes gathers its force and pushes into the present with an amazing burst of energy. Like a bomb. Or like something plunging off of a cliff. There was a traveler once who had such an experience. His name was Clay Richter. He went for a walk in the country, and stepped off the edge of the earth. He had a strange encounter with an alien force. Not the outer space kind of alien, but the surreal and perfect kind of alien, a mirrored self in a way, a shadowed self. Clay had that strange encounter with this alien self... this *other*... and it changed him. He'd had this strange encounter at precisely the moment in time when a revolution was sparked. He'd found a friend in the midst of his trial, an equal, a man named Volkhov. That meeting had changed him.

At this very moment, on a small patch of farmland in south central Pennsylvania, the world of Clay was gathering. These were people whom this traveler happened to meet on his journey. Clay Richter was no more, but in one way or another he was a part of the lives of these people who were now being drawn together.

It is not what you'd expect though. They did not know him in great detail. They knew him not exhaustively. They knew him as you might know the shoreline if you were floating downstream on a summer day. He'd been one of the many details in their lives, waving from the shore.

For example, as Clive and Red Beard sat in the drawing room waiting, they did not know that they each knew Clay.

Veronica and Stephen, who at that very moment were on their way through the gate of the farm complex, still amazed at this boy, Calvin, who had just saved them *again*... Veronica and Stephen did not know the men waiting in the house, and they could not know that those men knew Clay. And Calvin, of course, did not know Clay. He did, however, share in some ways his memory... and there was something else. Calvin was in Pennsylvania, having been sent on this adventure by Jonathan Wall. The books of Jonathan Wall had played a large part in setting Clay off on his journey.

All of the people converging on this farmhouse shared Clay, in some ways, but only through memory and circumstance. As a result, when they meet, they will not discuss him, at least not directly. Though they will be poorer for it, they will discuss him, if at all, in terms so vague that they will not be able to make him out. They will tell stories of a friend with whom they had once shared an apple, or a guy who had a real appreciation for Johnny Cash, or a guy who wrote these beautiful poems. But they will not speak of him. Not truly. They will not call him by his name.

And perhaps that is unimportant, after all. What is in a name? Would these friends of Clay not remember him just as tenderly, just as accurately, if they referred to him as Ned Ludd? Or Mr. Fugitive? The stories would probably all ring just as true for all these people.

No, the reason these people will not know Clay, will not recognize him even when they meet others who know him, is because they do not see him entire. They are like the blind men inspecting the elephant. One touches the belly and thinks he has found a wall, while another touches a leg and thinks he has a tree. Separately, none of them know exactly what they are dealing with.

So it is in the life of a man. There are things his fellows did know about him, but there were many other things they did not know. For example, they did not know, because they could not know, what had happened to the traveler. There was another man heading their way who had that piece of the puzzle. They did not know that Clay had been transformed by his contact with that *other* world, how he had met Volkhov as an equal. Nor did they know, because they could not know, that the traveler named Clay had a backpack that had traveled on without him. They did not know that the backpack, too, was on a journey.

Perhaps they can't be blamed, these friends of Clay, for their not knowing. And as they sit down in the drawing room together, where they will wait for... *What?* Gauguin? Godot? The set of boots and the backpack now trekking across the forest?

No. Now, as they sat in the drawing room and waited, they couldn't be held responsible for not knowing Clay better. They had each reached out to him on their brief sojourn with him, but he was a difficult man to know. You could prod him for answers, but he'd always take his time in getting you the answers. He was patient that way. You could ask him to hurry it up, but he'd just say "No."

# Chapter 17
# Team Warwick

Natasha and Lang huddled together in the kitchen as gunfire ripped through the building in waves, like music, or the ocean crashing against the beach in thunderous intervals. They held on to one another like one would hold on to a flotation device or a buoy if one was drowning in the violent ocean crashing around them.

At irregular intervals, Natasha would pop up and fire a round from the 9-millimeter pistol, but she was running out of ammunition. She looked Lang in the eyes with a look of pure affection, and then she jumped to her feet again and fired through the open window, expending the two final rounds that remained in the clip. She slumped back down next to Lang and looked at him again, still smiling.

"You're something else," he said.

"So are you, Lang."

"Well... we're something else then." He reached over with his right hand and clasped her hand in his. He gave the hand a light squeeze, and neither of them was anxious to let go.

"Do you suppose Elsie and Peter are alright?" she asked.

"I don't know. Things don't look particularly good for any of us right now."

"No. You're right."

"If they rush the place—" he let the words hang in the air, and did not complete the sentence.

"I know."

The two young people looked at one another, and their wordless communication was un-gilded, un-scripted, and unreservedly honest. The things that they did not say to one another were true, and they both meant them with all of their hearts.

Afraid that the opposing force might take the lull in fighting as an invitation to attack, Lang shuffled to his feet, and, balancing the barrel on the window frame, he popped off three quick shots from the .22, just to remind the enemy that someone armed was still in the cabin. It was a weak little protest, and it was met with a more powerful response. A bullet passed by Lang's ear so closely that it nearly took the appendage off. He dropped to the ground so fast that for a second, Natasha thought that he *had* been hit.

"Woah," Lang said, and laughed nervously. "That was close. They're getting better at this. I think they're timing our return fire."

\*\*\*\*

The round-faced man, like many in his tribe, bore many names. He decided on the spot that he preferred another. He was going back to being called Cole.

Cole made his escape while Mike and Steve were busy trying to locate the position of the sniper. Neither one wanted to move in any particular direction until they knew that they wouldn't be moving into the crosshairs of someone with an agenda different than their own.

The three Warwickians, Mikail, Sergei, and Vladimir had retreated back away from the ridge when Mikail indicated to the others that there was a sniper somewhere who was shooting at the National Guardsmen. The bulldog wordlessly ordered Val and Kent to circle around the ridge to the southeast in order to try to see who might be holed up in the cabin. This order gave Cole just the opportunity he'd hoped for.

Cole carried the new backpack as the group split in two. Just as soon as he and Vladimir had cleared Mikail's line of sight, Cole smoothly and fearlessly pulled the pistol from the band of his coat. He placed it to the back of Vladimir's head and pulled the trigger.

That was that. There was no ominous or threatening chit-chat. There were no syncopated rejoinders or catchphrases popping back and forth between the executioner and the executed. Cole was too smart for that stuff. He wasn't giving Vladimir an opportunity to weasel out of what he had coming.

Cole did not struggle within himself with the decision to kill Vladimir. He knew that Vlad was a coiled and poisonous serpent. A snake can and will strike anywhere and anytime. Vlad was a murderer many times over, and, as a cold-blooded psychopath, the man was too dangerous to suffer to live any longer.

In nature, rattlesnakes have a purpose. It is often said by people who are too ignorant to know better that "the only good snake is a dead snake." These people do not realize that if it were not for rattlesnakes, the human race would be wiped out by plagues and diseases from vermin in just a few years. Rattlesnakes are a necessary creature. We'd be lost without them.

But you don't let them into your bedroom where you sleep. Cole looked out through his glasses, and he noticed that they had some specks of blood on them. Those that get too close and won't go away, he thought, you have to kill. He pulled off the glasses and cleaned them on his shirt.

Perhaps Vladimir had a purpose. He'd never been a good person, or even a morally neutral person. He'd always been purely evil. He was, Cole figured, a rattlesnake that wouldn't leave the house. It was time for him to die.

Cole was now moving slowly, crawling foot by foot towards the rear of the cabin, when he inexplicably heard a voice from some bushes.

The bushes were calling to him using Peter's voice.

But they were calling him using his *real* name.

\* \* \* \*

"Do you ever wonder what life might have been like for us if..." Natasha stopped herself before she finished the question.

"If what?" Lang asked.

"...If we'd been from somewhere else... anywhere else... anywhere but Warwick?"

"I do wonder that, Natasha. I've thought about that a lot as we've traveled on this little adventure of ours. But..." he squeezed her hand softly as he tried to form the words to say the things he wanted to say. "But, I can't say that I would ask for anything to be different. Not a thing. Not even being here, right now, with you. I've thought about this a lot, Natasha... really I have." Lang reached up and touched Natasha's face, and just then a tear escaped her eye and traced its way down to where his hand rested against her cheek.

"How can you say that?" she asked, but with no hint of agitation or irritation at all. She really and truly wanted to know. "How can it be that you wouldn't change things if you could?"

"Because... I'm free now, Natasha. I realized it back when I got shot crossing Highway 17 a lifetime ago." Lang paused for a moment, and looked deeper into Natasha's eyes. "*'Not everything has a name. Some things lead us into a realm beyond words.'* Solzhenitsyn said that. I don't know that I can explain why I have joy and peace at this moment. I know Volkhov felt the same thing when he was in that prison with Clay in Warwick. When I was shot, I knew then that, for the first time in all of my life, I was moving, and breathing, and deciding... all as a free man. I just wonder... if none of this had happened, if I'd ever have really experienced freedom."

The gunfire from outside had slowed considerably, and Lang hesitated for a moment, afraid that the soldiers outside might be considering a raid on the cabin. He looked up and found that Natasha was still looking at him... as if she expected him to continue. So he did.

"I remember that man Clay. The one who accidentally stumbled into Warwick during the winter storm. He was looking for freedom, too. I'm not talking about political freedom, here particularly. I'm talking about *moral* freedom, the freedom to not be a puppet in another man's game, and I believe that Clay died happy, even if he was confused by all of it. He died saying 'no' to tyranny and wickedness. Just like Volkhov said. To me, it is okay to die, as long as you are doing it while acting out your freedom.

"So, no, I don't wish things had been different. I'm just glad that things worked out so that I could team up with you and Peter and Elsie... and Cole. I'm just glad that we all made the decision to say 'no.' I'm glad we had the courage to flee the system that was lying to us and enslaving us."

Natasha looked at him and smiled. The mention of Cole's name struck her a bit like a needle pushed into her skin, but she understood Lang's words, and she liked it that Lang said them to her. Another tear ran down her face, and she looked down before speaking again.

"If..." she paused for a moment, gathering her thoughts before beginning again. "If things *were* different. If we'd been born in a regular American town, and if we knew nothing of Russia or spies or any of this mess... well... Vasily Romanovich Kashporov... in such a case, I would love you anyway." She looked up at Lang, and he smiled.

Lang was just about to reply to Natasha, when he saw movement near the back door of the cabin. Cole rushed through the door, and Lang hardly had time to recognize who it was and stop himself before firing at the figure moving towards them. He did hold his fire, but the Missouri National Guard did not.

Seeing the movement in the cabin, the assaulting force opened fire again, and Natasha dove towards Cole dragging him down to the ground as a cascade of bullets smashed through the structure, destroying everything in their paths.

Simultaneous with Natasha's dive towards Cole, Lang sprung up again, instinctively, to offer covering fire, and rapidly squeezed off the four remaining shots left in the tube magazine of the squirrel rifle. Once again, his appearance was answered with a barrage of fire through the window, and once again, Lang dropped to the ground instantaneously with a loud thud.

Cole found Natasha on top of him, and he struggled to wiggle out from beneath her. He was worried that she'd been shot, and, as he struggled to get free, her head swung around towards his and their eyes met... and she smiled.

"Hello, brother," she whispered. "You okay?"

"Yes! Are you?" Cole replied.

"Yes. Not hit. Let's get into the kitchen though. It's safer."

The two low crawled back into the little kitchen area, and there they found Lang—Vasily Kashporov—slumped down with his back against the wooden cabinets.

He'd been shot through the throat, and he was dead.

\* \* \* \*

All of the Warwickians, those who were left among the living there on the field of battle, could not have known that they had just participated in a reunion of sorts. There wasn't any time to pause the action to notice. Peter, Cole, Natasha, Mikail, and Steve were still alive. Vasily and Vladimir were now dead. None of them knew the scope of the battle in which they now found themselves.

From high above the battlefield it could be seen that the Missouri National Guardsmen were receiving reinforcements in their positions opposite the tiny little cabin. Panning to the east, one might have seen that a large contingent of the FMA—the Free Missouri Army—was joining the battle against the MNG. A quick calculation would have given you the proper conclusion. *Peter and Elsie were trapped between the two opposing armies.*

Peter and Elsie were waiting, hoping, and praying that Cole would bring Natasha and Lang out of the cabin... but as they hoped, they became surrounded by the advancing FMA. Unarmed and not able to fight, they were forced by the FMA units to retreat behind their lines. They implored the soldiers to try to save Lang, Natasha, and Cole inside the cabin, but all they got were assurances that "everything that is within our power... will be done."

The FMA tried valorously to hold back the Missouri Guard from taking the cabin. There was a ferocious firefight.

All the while, Ace was off in the distance, doing his best to keep the Guard away from the cabin with his sniper rifle.

\* \* \* \*

Shortly after the FMA was forced to retreat back towards Lancaster County, the cabin was taken by the Missouri Guard.

Ace, out of ammo and unable to do anything else to save the people in the cabin, retreated with the FMA. It wasn't a difficult decision to make. He'd seen what the Missouri Guard had done to his hometown of Scranton. There was something in his memory about the way the smoke had curled up in little wisps over the house that had belonged to Irene Ducillo that made him angriest.

\* \* \* \*

# A WEEK LATER

Peter, Elsie, and Ace reluctantly left the FMA camp, and with beleaguered faces and sad countenances they set off on foot towards Amish country. The days of waiting for Natasha, Cole, and Lang to join them had sapped them of their emotional strength, and Peter finally decided that they could wait no longer.

The men of the FMA had been kind and helpful—at least as kind and helpful as they could possibly be under the circumstances—but it had become obvious that FMA leadership wanted the three travelers to either fight with them, or move along. They didn't have the materials or resources to keep refugees with them.

All-in all, it was time to move on.

The three said goodbye to their friends in the FMA and thanked them earnestly for their help and support. They left descriptions of their missing friends, and silently hoped that the three would be found safe and sound, and that they would rejoin them in the not-too-distant future.

And so, they walked. As they did, they talked about where they were going, and where they'd been. Well... actually... Peter and Elsie talked. Ace rarely said a word. He was a quiet man, and he talked more with his eyes and his actions than his words. He believed that actions spoke louder than words.

"We have to just keep moving," Peter said, trying to make his voice sound hopeful and authoritative. "If our friends are safe and alive, they'll know where we're headed, and we'll see them again."

"I know," Elsie replied. "I just can't help thinking that we might have all made it out of there *safely*, if only I'd stayed and helped Natasha move Lang."

Peter stopped and looked over at Elsie with a stern look. "We've talked about this, Elsie, and you know what I've said. This is no time for self-recrimination. We've all made decisions we now regret. We all could have done things differently. This world is falling apart and it will only get worse and—"

Just as he said those words, there was a sharp flash of light in the air. The ground rumbled violently. Seconds later, an indescribable wave of sound reached them and it shook through them as they walked. The general brightness in the sky seemed to gather in the east.

Instinctively, they all looked eastward, in the direction from which it seemed the noise had come. They were just above the tiny town of Bloomsburg, and they were approaching Interstate 80 from the north, and they had to move a few steps to their southeast to see it. When they did, they grew silent, and the three of them watched the top of it. It was like life and death personified. The mushroom cloud swelled in the distance to the southeast. It grew and expanded above the treeline.

Elsie shifted Lang's backpack on her back as Peter whispered. He whispered softly, but Ace and Elsie both could hear him...

"Philadelphia."

\*\*\*\*

Natasha and Cole stood in line to be processed into the Carbondale prison camp. They'd been captured by the Missouri National Guard and a fluke of circumstance had saved their lives. Rather than be executed on the spot, they'd been saved by the fact that there were no living officers on site to make that decision. Cole had told their captors that he'd only just arrived in the cabin at the very end, and that his sister didn't know how to fire a gun. Subsequently, they'd been arrested, and after they'd been loaded into a horse-drawn wagon full of prisoners bound for Carbondale, the circumstances of their arrests had been forgotten. Now, they were only potential laborers, and no one down the line cared what they'd been doing when they were captured.

"NATASHA JOHNSON!" the clerk shouted over her shoulder as she looked up at Natasha. That was the name she'd been given. No one had identification anymore. For those that did, it wasn't particularly helpful.

Someone behind the clerk wrote down the name, and then handed the clerk a form that explained where Natasha was to be billeted, and what her new occupation would be. Natasha took the form and stepped to the side to wait for her brother.

"COLE JOHNSON!" the clerk bellowed. Again, she was handed a form that she then handed to Cole. He looked at the form...

Barracks 19W
Garbage Detail

*Typical*, he thought.

\* \* \* \*


Cole rejoined Natasha, and they had just turned to leave when they both heard another clerk shout from two tables over.

"MIKE BAKER!"

Cole froze. He turned just in time to see Mikail receive his orders from the clerk.

"STEVE TAYLOR!" Sergei received his billeting as well.

Natasha and Cole stepped out of the tent and stopped to look at one another. They didn't know exactly what to think about what was happening, but they were both happy to be alive.

Just as the siblings looked down to their orders again, Mikail and Sergei walked up and Mikail smiled... sweetly, as if nothing had ever happened between any of them.

"Ahh, look Steve, some Warwick friends. How are you both?"

No answer.

"Where have they assigned you to live, Cole?" Mikail asked, innocently.

"19W," Cole said flatly.

"Fantastic," Mikail, replied. "It looks like we three Warwick men will be roommates. It'll be like home, won't it, Steve?"

Steve just nodded. His face did not betray his thoughts at all.

\* \* \* \*

The four Warwickians had just turned to walk away when it happened. They did not feel the ground shake or hear the noise from the explosion. Perhaps the geography was different in Carbondale, or perhaps the terrors of the place blocked out some input from the senses. It is impossible to tell for sure, since a person cannot be in two places at one time.

Someone—they could not recall who—shouted and pointed off to the southeast. The four turned as one and looked up into the sky. They watched as the mushroom cloud bloomed outward, just above the horizon.

Mikail Mikailivitch Brekhunov did not smile and he did not laugh. He just turned to his friend Sergei and said...

"Well, now. It seems that our friends have arrived."

*An Empty Bed, by C.L. Richter*

*Rarified hope, in darkness wanting*
*Vivified breath, breathless by haunting,*
*In day springs new*
*the way things do*
*When light shows false*
*night's cruel taunting.*

*Clarified dreams, by reality cleansed*
*When terrified streams of fear intends*
*By night to make*
*thy horrors wake*
*And strings burned through*
*bring forth earth's ends.*

# A Note

Due to all of the awesome support from WICK fans, we've arrived here at the end of the third "knot" in the story. We have one more knot to go.

Please <u>follow us on Facebook</u> so you can keep in touch with us and receive updates on the progress of the series.

We hope that you've made it this far because you enjoy the story, and we also hope that you'd like to see it become more popular so that more people will know that it exists. You've heard us say this before, but we really need help, so we'll say it again...

The *WICK series* is an independently published work. That is a fancy way to say that we don't have a handy agent or publisher with the means to market it properly. The only way it will ever find its way into the hands of readers is if those people who read it and enjoy it will become a part of the team and help us get the word out that it exists. We've done our part, we think. We've made it inexpensive so that it can be an easy and worthwhile purchase, and now we ask you to help get it out to more people.

The single most helpful thing that you can do to help us get the word out about W1CK is to review the book. It's free for you to do so, and if you enjoyed it, it is an excellent way to let other people know what you thought. So, we are asking you to PLEASE, while it is still fresh in your thoughts, go to Amazon.com or wherever you purchased the book and write a review for it. Your review doesn't need to be long, just a paragraph will do. You may not think a single review will help or hurt a book's probability of finding success, but if you think that, you are wrong. It is a fact of the modern market, that books that have more reviews, sell more copies, and have more credibility.

We've been heartened by the wonderful response to the *WICK* story, and it is your feedback and help that gives us the motivation to keep going. If enough people will get involved and help spread the news, we'd love to share more of the story.

We would also be very pleased if you would share links to *WICK* on Facebook, Twitter, and everywhere else on the Internet where such things are shared and discussed.

If you want to keep up with the *WICK* story, we've made a handy Facebook page for you...

http://facebook.com/wickbook

A *WICK* fan has also set up a WICK discussion page. If you are interested, please check it out:

https://www.facebook.com/groups/543889328956512/

Thank you so much for all of your help and support.

*Michael Bunker*

http://facebook.com/wickbook

Book Two of the *WICK* Saga... *now available!*

<u>*W1CK 2: Charm School*</u> *by Michael Bunker and Chris Awalt*

Book One of the *W1CK* Saga... *now available!*

*W1CK*, *by Michael Bunker and Chris Awalt*

Book One of The Last Pilgrims saga... *now available!*

*The Last Pilgrims, by Michael Bunker*

Now Available!

Make sure to be looking for Book Two of The Last Pilgrims saga...

*Cold Harbor, by Michael Bunker*

Coming Soon!

# About Chris Awalt:

Chris Awalt is a middle-aged man who rides a bicycle. He is also the father of two artful young daughters where he lives along the Jersey Shore. He is a freelance writer and a carpenter. His writing can be found on Andmagazine.com, where he writes columns on politics and culture, and chilledart.com, where he and his daughters manage a website on artful living. He can be found on both facebook and twitter.

Chris Awalt can be reached:
lchrisawalt@gmail.com

# About Michael Bunker:

Michael Bunker is an off-grid farmer, author, historian, philosopher, iconoclast, husband, and father of four living children. He lives with his family in a "plain" community in Central Texas where he reads and writes books... and occasionally tilts at windmills.

Michael Bunker on Facebook:
http://facebook.com/michaelbunker

Michael's Twitter:
http://twitter.com/mbunker (@mbunker)

mbunker@michaelbunker.com

# Other Books by Michael Bunker

<u>Futurity</u>, by Michael Bunker (2013)

<u>W1CK</u>, by Michael Bunker (2012)
ISBN 9781481858342

<u>W1CK 2</u>, by Michael Bunker (2012)
ISBN 9781482605532

<u>The Last Pilgrims</u>, by Michael Bunker (2012)
ISBN 9780578088891


Michael Bunker constrains most of his communication to *"snail mail"* (traditional post). Please write him a letter if you have questions, comments, or suggestions.

M. Bunker
1251 CR 132
Santa Anna, Texas 76878

Made in the USA
Columbia, SC
21 October 2021